SURVIVE THE FALL

POWERLESS WORLD

DEREK SHUPERT

STAND ALONE
SENTRY SQUAD

DEDICATION

I wouldn't be able to write without those who support me. I thank you for your encouragement and being there for me.

To those that read my books, I thank you for your support.

PROLOGUE

Once more into the fray, into the last good fight I'll ever know.

Russell Cage didn't want to die, but it wasn't his call. The plane was going to crash, and he was helpless to stop it. His fate was bound by luck, and the skilled hands of his best friend, Tim.

The nimble, lightweight aircraft dipped toward the mountains that were coated in lush trees. The torrid wind punished the plane as it fell from the sky.

Russell gulped, then closed his eyes.

The weightlessness of free-falling tickled his stomach. He felt nauseated. The bitter taste of acid burned the back of his throat.

A slew of regrets and words not spoken swelled in his head. He had unfinished business that would never be taken care of.

Tim fought the yoke, trying to keep them out of the blanket of rich vegetation for as long as he could. The tips of the pine trees punished the belly of the aircraft as it dipped below the canopy.

Branches snapped and wood splintered as the plane tore through the forest. The groaning of tortured metal filled the cabin. The propeller ripped from the front of the aircraft. Black smoke vented from the damage.

Tim gnashed his teeth and growled.

Russell pressed his hand against the dash while grabbing the hand grip with the other. He drew a sharp breath as he braced for impact.

The aircraft rattled and jolted the two frightened men. Sounds of panic fled their trembling lips as the front of the plane dipped further into the trees.

The windshield spiderwebbed, then busted as limbs hammered the cockpit.

Tim released his hold from the yolk and shielded his face.

Outside air flooded the cabin. The horrifying crescendo of the plane being ripped apart played in Russell's ears.

A thick bough breached the fuselage on the starboard side as the plane rolled clockwise. Luggage dumped from the gaping hole.

Russell closed his eyes, and thought of his wife, Sarah, hoping she knew how much he loved her. He had made many mistakes in his life, most of which he feared he'd never be able to rectify.

CHAPTER ONE

RUSSELL

TWENTY-FOUR HOURS EARLIER

S ome people find happiness in life. Others at the bottom of a shot glass. For Russell, it was more of the latter.

Another shot of whiskey went down the hatch. He had lost count after the sixth, or was it the seventh, shot that found its way into his stomach. By then, it didn't matter. He wasn't drinking for enjoyment. He was drinking to forget.

"Reload," Russell barked at Nate, the grizzly bartender that kept the drinks coming.

He gave Russell a pensive stare as he retrieved the empty shot glass from the scarred bar top. "Rough day at work?"

Every day was rough, regardless of where Russell was. It had been a year to the day since that home invasion. The day Jess, his daughter, was shot and killed by that ex-con who decided to break into their house and ruin his life forever.

Russell shrugged, then puffed on the cigarette that hung from his lips. "Not any worse than the other 364 days. Just trying to make it through this miserable existence as best I can."

Nate placed a clean glass in front of him. Russell twisted the top off the bottle of Jack he had been pounding away on for the better part of the night.

Nate shot Russell a glance as the end of the bottle dangled over the rim. "I'm calling it. Last round for you. After this, you're done."

Whatever. Just pour the damn whiskey.

Russell rolled his eyes, then twirled his fingers. He was growing impatient as he sighed, and stared at the empty shot glass. He needed his medicine.

The stout, brown liquor poured like a free-flowing river. Russell focused on the opening of the bottle, inhaling the smooth, smoky sweetness that he had grown to love as it sloshed into the glass. He licked his lips from the anticipation.

The alcohol vanished as fast as Nate served it. There was no sipping or savoring the beverage. Russell just needed to dull the pain of his daughter's death, to numb the guilt that had latched onto him like a leech.

He slammed the glass down on the counter, then leaned back on the barstool. His head swam in a sea of liquor and bad memories from the past year. He couldn't escape either, regardless of how much he tried or drank.

The cigarette was reduced to nothing more than a stump that fit between Russell's lips. He smashed the tiny bud in the ashtray nearby and blew the smoke from his mouth.

Nate leaned on the bar with both hands flat on the top. He nodded toward the restroom. "Since you're cut off, I think it might be wise for you to get a cab, and head home before you find trouble. Speaking of which, I think trouble's looking at you right now."

Russell rubbed his weary, glassy eyes, then glanced down to the end of the bar at the blonde who was looking his way. She took a sip of the margarita she was nursing and winked at him.

Nate was right. She had trouble plastered all over her. The temptress was glammed up with a heaping dose of makeup. It wasn't too much to make her look like a clown, but enough to make any honest man do a double take.

Her white dress clung to her hourglass frame as if it were painted on her toned body. The fabric was so tight that it left nothing to the imagination. Her full, puffy lips were coated with a dark-red lipstick, and her eyes were an icy blue that drew you right in.

Russell had spotted her the moment she stepped inside The Metal Flea Pub an hour or so ago. All of the other patrons of the pub gawked, and stared at the vixen as the pompous looking business type she was with paraded her to the opposite end of the bar. It was difficult to tell if they were a couple or if he had bought a block of her time.

"Hard pass," Russell spoke with a slight slur to his speech as he looked at Nate with shiny, bloodshot eyes. "Not my type. Besides, that's the furthest thing from my mind at the moment."

Nate pushed away from the bar top, then grabbed the empty shot glass from in front of him. "You might have to tell her that. She's heading this way."

She strutted down alongside the bar with her drink clasped in her hand from the corner of his eye. It was unclear why she even wanted to speak with him.

The day had beaten him into the ground, both physically and mentally. A twelve-hour shift at a security job he couldn't stand, and the death of his daughter bore down on his slouched shoulders.

Besides, the woman wasn't Russell's type. No one was except for his wife, Sarah. Sure, he had needs, but he only wanted her to fulfill those. That wasn't going to happen anytime soon, if ever, seeing as they had been separated for almost six months now, and divorce was looming on the horizon.

The woman's perfume arrived before she did, making Russell's head throb that much harder. He jammed his fingers into each socket and rubbed them.

She sat her drink on the counter, then asked, "Is this seat taken?"

"It's a free country, lady. Sit where you please. I'm leaving." Russell sat there with his elbows resting on top of the bar as he fought to keep the world from spinning.

She sat in the chair and leaned against the brass railing that ran the length of the bar while facing him. "No need to rush off so soon. We just started—"

Russell held up his hand, cutting her off before she could annoy him any further. "Listen, lady, no offense, but I'm not interested in what you're selling. I've had a long, tiring day, and I just want to be left alone. Besides, I can assure you that I'm not your type, and I don't have the money to procure your services."

She scoffed at the insulting comment. "Excuse me? Did you just insinuate that I'm a prostitute?"

Russell shoved his hand into the pocket of his trousers. He pulled out a wad of crumpled up bills, and cherry picked out what he needed to pay Nate.

He tossed the money on the bar. "Thanks, as always, Nate. See you next time."

"Want me to call you a cab?" Nate inquired as he grabbed the money.

4

Powerless World

Russell shook his head. "Don't bother. I'll walk. It's not that far. I could use the fresh air."

The woman droned on about the slanderous comment Russell made as he spun in his chair and stood up. Her voice grew with anger the more she spoke. He ignored her just the same.

The world was unbalanced as Russell took a moment to gather his bearings. He held his hands out to either side to stabilize his waning posture. He stumbled toward the exit of the establishment, wanting to put as much distance between him and the yapping vixen as possible.

Russell trudged out of the pub, and into the brisk, cool night that nipped at his exposed flesh. It felt good against his heated skin. Consuming the lot of whiskey, coupled with the reminder of his daughter's death, had done enough to stoke his fire.

His car was parked just around the corner on the far side of the pub. He hadn't planned on walking home, or drinking as much as he did, but things changed.

The door flung open behind Russell as he slumbered down the sidewalk. Angry voices bickered and grew louder.

"Yeah. That's the guy who called me a whore," the vixen yelled.

Heavy footsteps tromped his way. "Hey, asshole. Did you call my girl a whore?"

Russell had no desire to get into a confrontation with some rich snob. He dug his hands into his coat pockets, and continued on his way.

"Can you believe the nerve of this guy," the agitated man grumbled as he charged him.

"Steve, forget it," the vixen called out. "He's drunk and a loser, anyway. Don't waste your time."

Yeah, Steve. Just forget about it, Russell thought to himself.

"Screw that," Steve barked as he grabbed Russell's arm. "Nobody calls my girl a whore. Especially some low-life gutter trash."

Russell stopped dead in his tracks. He looked down to the man's hand that was fixed around his bicep. His fingers dug into the muscle and held firm.

"Listen, pal," Russell growled with slurred speech. "I didn't say your girl was a whore. I just insinuated it since, well, she's dressed for the part and far out of your league."

Steve snarled, then jerked Russell about to face him. The sudden movement threw Russell's head into a tailspin. He stumbled about with his hands out to counter the dizziness. He regained his composure just as Steve poked him in his chest.

"Apologize to her right now, and perhaps, I won't mop the sidewalk with your face," Steve said.

Russell battled the disequilibrium that consumed his head as he struggled to focus on Steve. He closed his eyes and stood still as Steve jabbed at his chest. This wasn't his first drunken stupor, or skirmish.

"Touch me again, and I'll lay you out," Russell warned. "Just go back inside with your slut girlfriend, and we'll call it a night, all right."

Steve gnashed his teeth and balled his hand into a fist. He grabbed a handful of Russell's coat and drew his arm back. Russell blinked, trying to erase the double vision. Two Steve's stood before him, ready to pound his face into oblivion.

Time slowed to a crawl. He had it all figured out. He'd dodge Steve's right cross, and counter with a jab to the stomach, then, knee him in the face. The perfect plan.

Powerless World

Steve swung his arm with everything he had and connected with the end of Russell's jaw. The blow knocked him off balance and sent him flat on his ass. Russell's eyes rattled in his head like loose marbles. It was a decent strike, but Russell had been dealt worse.

Russell rubbed his jaw while staring at the proud alpha who strutted back to his woman with his chest out. Russell wiped away the blood that trickled down from his chin. He wasn't looking for a fight, but watching Steve walk away, he had to wipe that smug grin from his face.

"You know, I have to admit, that's the weakest punch I have ever taken," Russell jabbed. "I think your woman there could hit harder than that."

Steve stopped and glanced over his shoulder. His cocky smirk vanished in a blink as his nostrils flared. Like a bull seeing red, he charged Russell once more, ready to dish out more pain.

Russell pulled himself off the ground as Steve closed the distance. His balance was still a bit shaken, but he would make do.

Steve drew his arm back, ready to strike the drunken fool who couldn't keep his mouth shut. "I'm going to mess you-"

Russell exploded from the sidewalk and decked him square in the face. Steve stopped on a dime and reeled from the punishing blow. Both hands cupped his bleeding nose as he squinted and howled in pain. Russell could've stopped and went on his merry way, but he didn't. He had a gut full of rage and heartache that needed to be vented, and Steve was the perfect source to unload on.

"Christ. I think you broke my nose," Steve yelled out.

His vixen raced to his side until she saw Russell stomping toward him. She paused and backed away. Her face twisted into sheer terror.

Russell punched Steve in the gut, doubling the businessman over in a snap. He grabbed him by the collar of his suit, then threw him against the brick wall of the pub. Steve collapsed, gasping for air. Russell kicked him in the stomach over and over as he glared down at him.

The vixen yelled and cried for help. She pleaded for Russell to stop, but her words fell on deaf ears.

Police sirens whistled in the night air.

The flash of red and blue on the aged brick wall gleamed in Russell's face, but he ignored them. He wasn't done yet.

"This is the police," a thunderous voice called out from behind Russell. "Break it up, now."

A baton slipped under Russell's chin. Arms wrapped around both of his and pulled him off the beaten businessman. Steve laid on the ground, coughing and hacking as two police officers dragged Russell to their squad car.

"What the hell," Russell barked as they threw him face first on the hood of their cruiser. "That dick bag started it."

"Yeah. Looks like you ended it, though," one of the officers said as he patted him down. "Have you been drinking tonight?"

"Some. Is that a crime?" Russell countered without thinking. It was a snide comment he wished he hadn't made. He was still amped up on adrenaline and booze.

"No, but until we get to the bottom of this, we're taking you two down to the station to cool off." The cop held his hands together as he fumbled with the cuffs on the side of his hip. He pulled them free and slapped them onto each of Russell's wrists.

CHAPTER TWO

SARAH

T he mounting loss of sleep had taken its toll. It was a fight that was lost more times than won. Insomnia was a bitch, no matter how you sliced it.

Sarah laid in bed and stared at the popcorn ceiling of her two-bedroom duplex for the better part of the night. The last time she checked, it was after midnight. Minutes passed like grains of sand slipping through an hourglass. She was helpless to stop it. She hated feeling that way, despite how hard she tried to turn the tide.

Being alone sucked.

She missed the warmth of a body next to her. The feeling of strong arms draped over her curvy frame in the dead of night that held her tight and made the world seem less scary. And, as she had learned, it was indeed a dreadful place.

Damn you, Russell. Why couldn't you have just tried a bit harder?

Sarah hated giving up, and pushing him away, but when one was at the end of one's rope, what else could one do?

The fight had been beaten out of her. Not physically, but emotionally. She felt dead inside. Besides, she was in competition against a formidable foe.

Tall, slender, and full of color, she paled in comparison to the rich taste of the poison Russell drowned himself on what seemed like a daily affair.

The grief of losing their daughter to that home intruder a year ago weighed heavily on everyone. It was a painful reality to accept, knowing that they'd never see her grow up into the amazing, young woman she was. The hardest part was not only losing her sweet girl, but the man she vowed to spend the rest of her life with.

Sarah squinted. Tears pushed out through the slits and rolled down either side of her flushed cheeks as she flipped over onto her side. She focused on the red hue of the digital clock on the oak nightstand like she was fixed in a trance.

Christ. It's 1:23 now.

If she didn't go to sleep soon, she'd pay for it in the morning.

Ding.

A text message dumped into Sarah's phone. The screen lit up, casting a wide swath of bright light that illuminated the dark corner of her cramped bedroom.

Sarah blinked and looked away from the blinding light as she reached for the phone. Confusion swirled in her head. Who would be texting her this late?

Her first thought was Russell drunk texting some gibberish garbage that wouldn't make any sense. Sarah couldn't stand that, and she'd told him as much. It had been some time since he had done it. Actually, it had been a long while since she had heard from him all together. When she'd had enough and told him to leave her be, that was the last words they had spoken to one another.

Powerless World

The number looked unfamiliar. It was local to the city, though. Area code 617, but that didn't mean much. Telemarketers were cunning with how they tried to get you on the phone to speak about your extended car warranty, but this late, it was doubtful that it was a telemarketer.

She thumbed the message, opening it up on the screen. It only took reading the first sentence to send a chill down Sarah's spine.

Why are you ignoring me?

It was Spencer, or as Sarah called him, the Creeper. He was a guy from a blind date she was set up on by her best friend, Mandy. She nudged Sarah into it, which was something she wasn't keen on. An innocent, friendly meetup with no expectations that had gone horribly wrong.

Spencer seemed nice enough at first, and acted the part of a polite and caring gentlemen, but when Sarah refused a second invite by the tall and reasonably good-looking guy, he changed. Like a Doctor Jekyll and Mister Hyde scenario, he was now one scary beast that lurked within the black matter of her brain. He refused to leave her alone.

A restraining order had to be put in place, and thus far, it had worked. He was sight unseen. Still, just the hint of his unsettling gaze made Sarah's skin scrawl. For an added level of protection, she bought a gun and got her conceal carry. She had no intent of using it, but if push came to shove, she wouldn't hesitate to draw the weapon, and pull the trigger.

Another message dropped, more visceral than the last. She looked away from the comment that made her sick to her stomach. Spencer wasn't getting the hint which made Sarah both angry and fearful.

"LEAVE ME ALONE. YOU KNOW YOU'RE NOT SUPPOSED TO BE CONTACTING ME," she typed, hoping he'd get the hint.

Sarah waited for a scathing response as she eyed the drawer of her nightstand. That's where she kept her Glock 43—well within reach if she needed it.

Seconds ticked by with no reply.

Sarah breathed a sigh of relief. She'd have to contact the police station during the day to inform them of what had transpired.

A disturbance from the rear of her house sent Sarah on edge. It sounded like the trash cans being knocked over. She gasped and tightened her fingers around the phone. Spencer was outside of her home.

Instinct kicked in as she yanked the drawer open to her nightstand. She didn't have to look inside or shine any sort of light into the well-organized drawer. Her hand went right to the Glock that sat ready.

Sarah grabbed the grip and pulled the Glock out. She trained the barrel at the blackness that loomed beyond her open door. Her heart pressed against her chest; each thump more intense than the last. She sucked in a deep breath of air, and released it slowly. She swallowed the fear that washed over her, tossed the covers from her legs, and slipped out of the warmth of the sheets to the slight chill of her house. She kept a keen eye on the hallway as she made her way around the bed.

The wood floor creaked with every step she took. She cringed from the sharp noise. Her hand trembled with the Glock. The closer she got to the door, the faster her heart raced.

Sarah paused, thumbed through her phone, and switched on the flashlight. The back lit up and chased away the darkness. She toed the entrance to her bedroom, then peered around the jamb out into the silent hallway. No footsteps or other audible noises were heard. Still, she wouldn't be able to sleep a wink until she swept her dwelling.

The stark white light washed over the cream-colored walls and the few photos she had up of her family. She peered into the second bedroom that was a cluttered mess of boxes, and other junk she hadn't messed with since moving in. She craned her neck and swept the space.

Another clatter from outside drew Sarah's attention back in the direction of the living room. She fought to control her breathing which escalated with every step she took. Terrible thoughts of Spencer lurking around her house played through her head. Him toying with her like some sick game of cat and mouse that she couldn't escape.

Sarah tiptoed through the murk of the living room toward the modest dining room. Two large windows looked out over the small scale fenced in yard. The trash cans were lined against the fence on the far side which she should be able to see from the corner of the window.

The blinds covering the windows were closed. Sarah skirted around the small, round dining table. Her finger repositioned over the trigger of the Glock, ready to fire if need be.

She peered into the small kitchen that was adjacent to the dining room for any shadowy figures that might be lurking within the gloom. The light from her phone swept the dark-blue countertops and light oak cabinets. It was clear.

Sarah pressed her shoulder to the wall next to the window. Her fingers parted the wooden blinds as she peeked out into the backyard. She craned her neck, and scanned over the area where she kept her trash cans, hoping she wouldn't find a dark clad figure lingering on her property.

There was no one there. The trash cans sat in the same spot she remembered leaving them. Perhaps she'd imagined it all. Afterall, lack of sleep could play tricks on one's mind.

The phone rang. Sarah jumped.

Christ.

She prayed it wasn't Spencer as she flipped the phone around to see the screen. It was the Boston Police Department. What did they want?

She lowered the Glock and answered the call. "Hello?"

Her gaze danced over the living room and kitchen as she listened to the officer on the other end.

"Hey, Sarah, it's David," the officer said. He was a long-time family friend of hers and Russell's.

"Hey. What's going on? Everything all right?" she asked.

"I just wanted to let you know that Russell was brought in," the officer said. "He got into a fight at a bar. He's sleeping it off in a cell right now. He didn't ask me to call you or anything like that. I just felt you should know and all."

Her head hung low as she sighed in frustration. Russell was in trouble yet again.

Sarah wanted nothing to do with it. If he lacked the willpower to fight the temptress that was his vice, he needed to cool off for the night in a jail cell. Perhaps it would give him time to reflect on the life he was living. She doubted any revelation would come to him, but stranger things had happened.

"Thanks, David. Just leave him there. Perhaps it'll do him some good."

CHAPTER THREE

RUSSELL

Russell woke to a splitting headache that bored deep into his skull. It had been some time since he had been that wasted. He hadn't missed it.

He was lying flat on his back. His bed felt hard and rigid. There was no pillow or sheets. No soft mattress that cradled him. Just a solid piece of wood that knotted the muscles in his back.

A stark light blasted him in the face as he fought to open his eyes. His hands shielded him from the harsh sunlight that forced him to look away. It took a moment for Russell to figure out where he was.

Jail. More so, the drunk tank.

"Long night, pal?" a raspy voice asked.

Russell grumbled in response. His legs fell from the wooden bench and dropped to the cement floor. He sat up and deflated against the cinder block wall. His head slumped back as his mouth slagged open.

"Yeah. You could say that," Russell muttered.

The stink from the man was stout. He smelled as though he hadn't bathed in forever. It was more than enough to bring Russell out of the drunken state he had been in.

"Who's Jess?" the man inquired as Russell fought to get his bearings.

Russell squinted. His face twisted into a scowl, and his lips pursed as he stared at the homely looking man. "What did you say, old timer?"

The man's eyes widened as he brought his unkempt hands up in the air. He scooted down the bench and away from Russell. "You were saying her name throughout the night. Just wondering who she was is all."

"Cage," a stern, authoritative voice barked from the other side of the cell.

Russell cut away from the hesitant drunk and stared at the officer. He stood up from the scarred wooden bench and schlepped toward him. Russell glanced back at the man with curious eyes as the cell door was unlocked.

"You're free to go," the officer stated as he swung the door open.

Russell left the cell and followed the officer out of the holding area. He gave the homeless man one last look before passing through the open doorway.

"For Christ's sake, Russell," a disappointed voice harped from behind. "I thought we were past this."

Russell didn't need to turn around to know who it was. The heavy sigh and judgmental undertone gave it away. "Hey, David."

The officer escorting Russell through the station looked past him.

"I'll take it from here, Frank," David said.

Frank nodded and glanced at Russell for a split second before walking away.

Russell dipped his chin and stared at the white-speckled linoleum floor. He scratched at the stubble that grew on the sides of his face. "I had a bad night. You know what day it is."

David placed his hands on his hips, then tilted his head. "Yeah. I know what day it is, but you're going to have to do a better job of keeping it together."

Officers passed by and skirted around them as they chatted in the middle of the hallway. Russell watched the uniformed men stare at him as they continued on their way.

David placed his hand on Russell's shoulder, then nodded down the hall. "Come on."

The two of them strolled through the police station and gathered Russell's belongings. David escorted him to the entrance of the building. They stepped outside to the brisk, cool morning air, wandered down the sidewalk, and stopped to chat.

"Thanks for getting me out of there," Russell said. "I owe you big."

David kept his gaze fixed on Russell. "Just add it to the laundry list of IOUs that you have stacked against you, which is growing by the way. Besides, it wasn't me who got you out. The suit you had a beef with told us he attacked you first. You should've stopped when you had him on the ground. You were lucky, again."

Russell nodded in agreement. The list of favors and strings David had pulled for him was long. Russell knew each instance where David had helped him out of a jam. He was lucky to have such a friend, but felt that luck would run out soon.

A black Tahoe pulled into the parking space near them. Russell glanced at the sparkling vehicle, and knew it was his best friend and closest confidant. "You called Tim?"

David nodded his head. "Yeah. Figured you could use a ride home."

"What about my car?" Russell countered. "It's still parked over at The Metal Flea Pub."

David nodded at Tim who waited in the vehicle. He looked like he was on the phone. "Just get it later. Go home. Get a shower, and get your crap together, brother. I don't want to see you in here again."

Copy that, Russell thought.

Russell shook David's hand and headed to the passenger side of the Tahoe. He opened the door and stepped up into the cab.

"Yeah, that won't be a problem," Tim spoke into the phone. "Text me the details, and I'll make sure it happens by Monday. Later."

Russell slammed the door while looking at Tim. "You didn't have to come down here to get me."

Tim tossed the phone into the cubby hole in the center console. He gave Russell a pensive stare. "Of course, I did. Not sure who else would've come and picked your drunk ass up."

Russell held up his hand. "I'm not drunk anymore. A bit hungover, maybe, but that's it."

"Gotcha. Well, you're batting a thousand for sure," Tim replied as he put the SUV into reverse. "Might need to stop and get some lotto tickets."

Russell grabbed the seat belt and pulled it across his chest. He fastened it in place as Tim backed out onto the street. "Why is that?"

Tim smirked. "Because you're one lucky son of a bitch."

He shifted the truck into drive and punched the gas.

Powerless World

The ride back to Tim's condo was a quiet drive. Russell kept his gaze focused out of the passenger side window and watched as the businesses and houses flew by. He didn't feel like chatting about what had happened, or the utter mess his life was in. He knew things had to change, or he was destined to live in the black hole of despair that was his existence.

"Damn it," Russell groaned with a heavy sigh.

"What is it?" Tim probed as he looked his way.

"I had the early morning shift today at Teledyne. My boss is going to go berserk when I call, and tell him I'm running late. He's probably going to fire me." Russell rubbed his eyes, then rested his elbow on the side of the door.

"You hate that job," Tim stated. "You've been talking about quitting there for months. Would it be so bad if it happened?"

That was true. Russell hated working at Teledyne as a security guard, but it was a job. One that he needed. "Yeah, well, since money doesn't grow on trees and I'm loafing on your couch, I kind of need to get my act together. I was only supposed to stay with you for a short stint. I feel bad that it's gone on much longer than it should have."

"It's not a problem at all. I've told you as much. You can stay as long as you need to. Mi casa es su casa." Tim dismissed the thought with a wave of his hand as he turned down Blanchet Street. His condo wasn't much farther, which made Russell happy. A nice hot shower was calling his name.

Russell smiled, then nodded. "Thanks. I owe you."

Tim pulled alongside the curb and stopped in front of a dark-brown brick building. He placed the Tahoe into park and winked. "As stated before, I'll just put it on your tab."

Russell gave a wry grin as they got out of the SUV.

They walked across the sidewalk, and through the archway that led up a flight of stairs to Tim's abode. Russell checked his phone for any messages that he may had gotten from Sarah while sleeping off another mistake in the clink.

There were no texts or missed calls from her. It didn't surprise him, but he'd hoped she would've reached out, considering what day it had been.

He did have a missed call and a message left by his work. Great.

Russell played the voicemail, which was as he expected. He was terminated, effective immediately. A bit harsh, but the news didn't surprise him. He knew he was on his boss's last nerve.

"When's the last time you heard from her?" Tim asked as he fumbled with his keys.

Russell ended the message, then slid his phone into the back pocket of his work trousers while Tim unlocked the door. "Too long. A couple of months, I think."

"Give her some time, man. She'll come around."

Tim slung open the door and stepped inside his spacious condo. Russell followed him in. Tim tossed his keys on the counter, then turned to face Russell.

Russell rubbed his hand up and down his face. He slipped off his coat and tossed it over the couch. He caught Tim staring at him while leaning against the bar. He looked like he was ready to do a deep dive into the mess that was Russell's life. Russell had no desire to do that.

"No offense, but I've already chatted with David this morning about my recent actions," Russell said. "Diving into it again isn't high on my list of things to do. Besides, I don't bust your balls all the time about how much you smoke, do I?"

Powerless World

Tim tilted his head in agreement. "You don't, but we did agree to keep the other in check, and call them out if they were slipping. That's all I'm saying."

Russell sighed. Tim was right, but still, he wasn't in the mood for a lecture. "Can we wait until later before we talk about this? It's been a shitty twelve hours, and it doesn't look like it's getting any better. I lost my job."

A jovial smile slit across Tim's face. "This is great."

How was that good news? "Great? How do you figure?"

Tim pushed away from the bar and placed his hands on Russell's shoulders. "Because. We're taking a trip."

Derek Shupert

CHAPTER FOUR

SARAH

Sarah woke in a panic in the middle of her bed from the bad dream she'd had. She lifted from the mattress with the Glock and phone still clutched within her grasp. Her chest heaved in and out, and her pulse raced like a stallion at the derby.

The night's stressful dealings with Spencer texting and receiving a call from the police about Russell had kept Sarah on edge. The insomnia was bad enough without adding the Creeper and her husband to the fold.

Sarah blinked, trying to erase the film that coated her eyes as she surveyed her bedroom. The haze remained and made it difficult to see at first. Her knuckles dug into each socket as she blinked some more.

The Creeper wasn't there. Her room was void of any persons except for her. There were no strange sounds that loomed from any other part of her duplex either.

Thank God.

Sarah lowered the Glock, then tossed the weapon to the covers. She panted and fell back on the stack of plush pillows that cradled her body. Her eyes were sore from lack of sleep. They stung as she squinted. She dug her knuckles into each socket, trying to relieve the irritating sensation.

Her head fell to the side as she exhaled. The bold red letters of her digital clock made her grumble.

Great.

It was after 11 AM, much later than she had intended to sleep.

The early bird gets the worm was a saying her dad had drilled into her head from a young age. Sleeping the day away was a sin in his eyes. Time was valuable, and it needed to be used wisely. Plus, it gave her mind the opportunity to run wild, and think of all the horrid things that had gone wrong over the past week.

A full day had been planned out for her. Not by choice, but by her good friend, Mandy. Shopping, eating, and who knew what else. Sarah wasn't in the mood for such things, but she had put Mandy off for too long. The last time they spoke, Mandy made sure to remind her of that.

Sarah rolled out of bed and stretched her arms. A big yawn attacked her. She grabbed the Glock from the covers and stowed it back in its place within her nightstand drawer.

She trudged around her bed while checking her phone. It was a morning routine that was done daily without fault. Check the latest news out on social media, then a few entertainment sites to see what was going on in the world of movies and music.

The social media site she frequented was first up. She thumbed the app on the screen. A blue circle twirled as the site's logo splashed on the screen, but wouldn't load. An error popped up, informing her that the device didn't have a signal.

That's strange.

The bars in the top right corner of her phone showed up, then slipped away. A zero with a line throughout populated in the space. The WIFI she had was also on the fritz.

Par for the course.

Just more issues that seemed to mound up on an already rough morning.

Her shoulders sagged with the weight of a restless night as she walked out into the hallway. Every step seemed like a chore. Her feet felt like cinderblocks were shackled to her ankles. Coffee was what she needed, stat.

Sarah thumbed the power button to restart the phone. The manufacture logo splashed on the screen as she passed through the living room. If it didn't stop acting up, she'd have to take it in. Again.

The site of her Keurig made her smile. The rich aroma of the dark coffee grounds being cooked by the hot water made her mouth water.

A creature of habit, Sarah had her black mug stationed under the spout. No sugar or creamer was used. She liked it hot and black.

She powered on the unit and listened to the steady hum of the heating element flash boil the water in the reservoir. Her phone dinged, and fired up. She leaned against the counter and waited for the phone to finish loading as she yawned again.

Through one of the kitchen windows, Sarah spotted the trash cans and thought of Spencer.

Was that him outside of her house this morning? Had he been skulking about like some demon in the murk? He fit the bill which made Sarah shudder from the thought.

The lights on top of the Keurig flashed blue, indicating the unit was ready to be used. A cup of happiness was less than a minute away. She pressed the large, blue flashing button as her phone rang. It was Russell this time.

She stared at the screen, contemplating whether or not she wanted to answer. She was in no mood to fight, or talk about anything that dealt with their strained marriage. She had already checked out for the most part, and had been in talks with a divorce attorney about next steps.

The phone rang and rang. Sarah sighed, then answered the call.

"Hey." Her tone was lifeless and void of any pleasantries a lover would have toward her mate.

"Hey, ba-" Russell paused, not finishing the affectionate greeting he was used to. His voice was choppy. It sounded more like a robot. "Good morning."

Sarah folded her arms across her chest and tapped her foot, wishing it would make the call end sooner. "What do you want?"

"Long night?" Russell asked.

"You could say that."

"Couldn't sleep, huh? Insomnia still getting the better of you?"

"Among other things." The smell of coffee permeated Sarah's nose which made her turn toward the Keurig. She watched the dark liquid finish pouring into her mug.

Russell grew silent. He took a moment before responding. "Is that guy still bothering you?"

Powerless World

Sarah's eyes widened from shock. How did he know about Spencer? She didn't recall telling him, and that wasn't something she'd divulge to him anyway. "How do you know about that?"

Silence filled the end of the phone before Russell answered. "David told me some guy was giving you problems. Don't be mad at him. He just wanted me to know."

"Well, it's nothing for you to worry about. I can handle myself, and him." Sarah removed the mug. Steam lifted into the air. The heat radiating through the ceramic mug warmed her hands.

Russell sighed. "I know you can. You're tough and resilient. I just—worry is all."

Sarah took a sip of the torrid brew.

Russell cleared his throat. "Anyway, I just wanted to tell you that I am sorry about everyth—. I know I've been a—husband for—time and that you deserve better. I'm heading—town for the weekend with—and was hoping that when I—back, maybe we can talk some. I don't want—lose—Sarah."

The reception was getting worse. Sarah struggled to make out what Russell said before the line went dead. She pulled the phone away from her ear and looked at the screen. The signal had been lost again, and it didn't look as though it was coming back.

Sarah thumbed the different apps again while sipping her coffee. Each opened to the same error.

No service available.

What the hell?

Perhaps it was a glitch with the cell provider, or maybe their satellite had experienced a malfunction. Sarah didn't care. She just wanted a functional phone.

Sarah pocketed the phone in her robe and hauled the coffee back to her bedroom. Another big yawn overtook her as she cupped her mouth. The restless night's sleep and bad dreams Sarah was plagued by wouldn't let her be. Even now, it made her feel uncomfortable as she wrapped her arms across her chest. Despite trying to move on with her morning, the sensation remained.

A warm shower could help, at least Sarah hoped it would.

She spent the next hour or so taking a shower and getting dressed. Mandy was meeting her at Copley Place around twelve, so she was already running late and needed to move faster.

Dressed and ready to leave, Sarah rapped her fingers against the jamb of her bedroom door as she glanced back to the nightstand.

The Creeper lingered in the back of her brain. His unsettling text messages gnawed at her insecurities and wouldn't stop. Sarah felt confident she could handle herself if push came to shove, but having the Glock on her would make her feel more at ease.

Afterall, it was better to be safe than sorry.

Powerless World

CHAPTER FIVE

RUSSELL

If humans were meant to fly, they'd have wings.

Russell wasn't a fan of heights. It rattled his nerves and made his skin crawl. The thought of seeing the ground from an elevated view clawed at his stomach. He had enough worry in his life. He didn't need to add to it.

Tim knew as much, but still, he persisted on Russell flying to Virginia in his plane, for the weekend—clear his mind of all the issues that were weighing him down. Have some fun for a change without wallowing in the muck of his existence.

He was a great pilot, or at least he was still alive and hadn't crashed. Tim loved flying so much that he decided to sink all of his money, plus multiple loans, in the charter business he ran. He was a people person and smooth as ice which kept him knee-deep in women and on the go with various jobs. The man's life was never dull.

Powerless World

Having fun and time to unwind from the stress Russell had been fighting through was something Tim had been trying to get him to do for some time. His moment of weakness had now steered him in the direction of facing a lifelong fear.

A quick plane ride in Tim's Cessna 400. That's how he sold it to Russell, anyway. They'd be at their destination before he knew it.

Anything smaller than a jumbo jet, Russell viewed as a crop duster. The Cessna wasn't, but the lightweight aircraft and absence of interior space made it look like one.

Tim wouldn't divulge where they were heading. All he said was, "It'll be a surprise. You're going to love it, and you'll forget about the flying part of our excursion."

Russell had his doubts, but he trusted Tim, despite his own anxiety screaming in his skull to not go along. It could've been the Xanax or Ambien he had taken before they left for Logan International Airport that mellowed him out some. He was still a bit on edge, but the medicine helped curb the angst.

"I can't believe you talked me into this," Russell groaned as they secured the few bags they had in the aircraft. "Not sure whatever surprise you have in store is going to be worth flying in your crop duster."

Tim chuckled, then smiled as he looked at Russell. "Like I said, you'll be fine. It's only a couple of hours, if that. It'll pass by fast. Besides, you'll have some wonderful scenery to look at. It's an amazing view. Something you can't experience anywhere else in the world. I can promise you that."

Russell had his doubts. He could get the same view while watching the Discovery channel or some other nature show from the safety of a couch or chair at home. "If you say so."

Tim stepped away from the opening of the aircraft and looked at Russell. "All right. I think we're good to go. You ready?"

"You got anymore Xanax?" Russell countered.

Tim chuckled again, then shook his head. "I've got more for the way back, but I don't think you're going to need it. Like I said, once you're up there, you won't ever want to come down. It's life changing."

Russell rolled his eyes. That was an unlikely scenario. Tim might mean well, but Russell's view about planes wasn't going to change. "Don't kill us, all right?"

"I'll do my best," Tim jabbed while winking.

Not funny.

Tim touched Russell's arm, stopping him from boarding the plane. He dug his hand into the front pocket of his pants and pulled his lighter out. "Here. Hold onto this for me, will ya?"

Russell took the lighter, then asked, "Why?"

"New beginnings," Tim winked.

Russell nodded and shoved the lighter deep into the pocket of his jeans. For Tim, this was a big move, one that Russell would have to try and match.

They loaded into the cockpit and settled into the rich, tan leather seats. Russell stared at the dash as he fumbled with the seat belt. A slew of buttons, switches, and gauges outlined two large screens that were fixed before them. Off to the side of the dash was a control yoke. It looked like a gaming joystick, but Russell didn't want any part of it. He preferred his games not to be real, or thousands of feet in the air.

Tim pointed to the headset that hung from the corner above the dash, then to his ears. "Put that on, so it'll be easier for us to speak."

Russell grabbed the headset and slipped it over his head. The black cushioned ear pieces conformed to his ears. He dug his hand into the front pocket of his jeans and retrieved his phone as Tim did his preflight checklist.

Flight jargon spewed from Tim's lips as he spoke to the tower. It played as background noise as Russell opened his wallet to a picture of Sarah and Jess.

The world around him fell silent as the past played in his mind's eye. He wanted them both back, but those days of a happy life were out of his reach, and the odds of getting his wife back were a long shot. Russell hoped that when they returned, Sarah would give him a chance to speak, and perhaps, offer him one final chance with her.

"Hey, you ok over there?" Tim asked.

Russell nodded, then slipped his phone back into his pocket. "Yeah. Peachy."

The engine of the Cessna thrummed as Tim took them out onto the runway. He worked the control yoke like it was an extension of his body as his other hand adjusted dials on the dash. "What did Sarah say when you called her?"

Russell adjusted his bulk in the seat as the subtle bumps and vibrations caused him to grip the armrest a hair tighter. "Shouldn't you concentrate on what you're doing here and less on me?"

Tim dismissed the question with a flick of his wrist. "I can multi-task. I've done this so many times, I can probably do it in my sleep."

The off-handed comment drew a concerned look from Russell. His eyes widened and his mouth split apart. "Well, I'd prefer if you just stay focused on the task at hand for now."

Tim smiled and throttled the engine. The lone propeller on the front spun faster. The aircraft shuddered from the engine revving.

The plane took off down the runway at a good clip. Russell sunk into the leather seat and grabbed the armrest tighter as Tim pulled back on the control yoke. The tires left the safety of the earth, and they ascended into the clear blue sky.

"See, it's not so bad," Tim said as they climbed at a modest rate. "Still feeling all right?"

Russell gave a thumbs up as his hold on the armrest lessened.

The Cessna climbed for what seemed like forever before leveling out. Tim monitored the wall of gauges and readings before him as he nudged Russell's arm. "So, was Sarah on board with talking when we get back?"

Russell shrugged. "Not sure. She always sounds unhappy when I speak with her. Plus, my phone was acting strange. The signal was shotty. Cutting in and out. Worst possible time for that to happen."

"I have faith it'll all work out as it needs to. Just hang in there, and don't give up," Tim reassured.

Hang in there. Russell had been doing that for months. Even in the face of a looming divorce and a drinking problem, he hung by a mere thread that was his everything.

Minutes ticked by like seconds.

The rhythmic hum of the Cessna's engine played through the silent cabin of the aircraft. Russell wrestled with his fear and peered down to the sprawling forest below.

Tim wasn't wrong. The view was stunning, something he had never seen before in his life.

Off in the distance, mountains stood as the back drop to an already breathtaking scene. The peaks lifted to the sky, full of rich green texture. It was like a different world—one where the footprint of human civilization was minuscule compared to the city.

"This would've been amazing to see last night with as clear as the sky was," Tim mentioned.

Powerless World

Russell didn't follow. "What do you mean?"

"The Northern Lights," he clarified. "First time they've been pushed this far. I heard folks as far as Georgia were able to-"

Tim stared at the dash. A look of confusion washed over his face as he tapped the flickering screen.

"What's wrong?" Russell probed.

Tim didn't answer. His brow raised in confusion as he tapped the screen harder. He went through a battery of checks that spanned most of the gauges that were showing signs of failure. His hands moved from knob to switch in a blink. The lights dimmed, then flickered as if the power coursing to each was being cut off.

Tim cupped the palm of his hand over the headset. He listened close for a few seconds before ripping it free of his head. Russell followed suit and watched with a worried gaze as Tim continued adjusting the aircraft's controls.

"We seem to have lost navigation. Communications are gone as well."

"Stop messing around," Russell snapped. He wasn't in the mood for any games.

There was no smile or chuckle that came from Tim. Only a concerned look that Russell hadn't seen before. "I'm not messing around. We're losing power for some reason."

The engine sputtered. The plane dropped which pulled a frightened squelch from Russell. His heart punched his ribs, fighting to break through.

"Come on," Tim growled as the dash went dead. He flipped every switch and turned every knob, trying to get any of the onboard systems to respond. The gauges were void of power, the screens dark and absent of any light. The propeller wound down as the plane dipped toward the earth.

Tim checked his seat belt again. He tugged at the strap to ensure it was secured.

"On my God. Are we going down?" Russell muttered through the panic that swallowed him whole. He knew the answer, but hoped he was wrong.

As calm as he could, Tim cut his gaze over to Russell as he fought with the control yoke. "Make sure your seat belt is secured, and brace for impact. We're going down."

Powerless World

CHAPTER SIX

SARAH

Sarah arrived to Boylston Station as the scuffed gunmetal doors slammed shut on the subway. A second later and she wouldn't have made it inside.

She was out of breath, panting hard as the heels of her palms rested on the soft parts of her knees. The subway shuddered, then took off down the tunnel toward Copley Station.

It was a last-minute decision to ride the subway. Her truck had refused to start, and she didn't have time to investigate what issues where plaguing the aging, red eyesore.

Public transportation wasn't high on her list of modes of getting around Boston, but beggars couldn't be choosers.

The subway wasn't packed, at least not the section she was in. There were three other riders in the car aside from her. They looked as thrilled to be on the rickety subway as her with long faces and emotionless gazes staring off into space.

Their dipped chins lifted and trained in her direction. Odd stares stuck to Sarah like a bad stench as she sat down in one of the open seats. Her hair was a bit of a mess as she ran her fingers through the strands, trying to straighten it out as best she could.

Small beads of sweat populated Sarah's brow and raced down her face. She waved her hand, trying to cool the flushed skin. She could've waited the extra thirty minutes for the next subway, but time wasn't on her side.

"In a rush, dear?" an elderly woman asked from the seat across from Sarah. She offered a warm smile that was swallowed by numerous wrinkles across her aged face.

Sarah shrugged, then smirked at the comment. "Story of my life."

The woman raised her hand from the black cane she had nestled between her legs. She pointed at Sarah and shook her skeletal finger as if to scold her.

"I hope to the lord above you're not chasing after some man, sweetie. You are too beautiful to have to do that. Those men should be chasing after you."

You have no idea.

"Just running late to meet a friend, is all," Sarah clarified. "Cell reception has been crap today, and I wasn't able to reach her. Not sure what is going on."

"I noticed the same thing," a larger woman across the car spoke out. Her black hair was pulled back into a ponytail with loose, wiry strands that stuck out from the sides of her head. She straightened them, then pulled the unruly hairs behind her ears. "I was trying to call my son's worthless father and couldn't reach him. At first, I thought he was just ignoring my calls, then I tried my best friend, and couldn't reach her either."

The two other passengers on the car nodded in much the same way. It didn't sound like her phone was the issue, but instead, the cell service wasn't working for whatever reason.

The lights overhead flickered. The passengers glanced to the dull, monotone lights that cast the interior in a pale shade of white, then rolled their eyes.

"The city needs to upgrade these subway systems," the elderly woman barked. "It isn't safe to be underground with the way those lights flicker, and the horrible noise the subway makes."

A homely, middle-aged man, seated a few sections down from the large woman, sighed. He ran his large hand over his thinning hair. His fingers then balled into fists and his lips pursed which made Sarah uneasy.

He glanced her way with his brow furrowed and nostrils flaring. "About like everything else in this God forsaken city. Subpar accommodations for the taxpayers who are forced to take such means of transport."

Sarah kept silent and avoided engaging the disturbed man. Besides, she didn't have an opinion on the matter she wanted to share. Sarah wasn't a regular rider of the subway. It was something she'd have forgone if she could have.

Damn truck.

The lights flickered again, then crashed, thrusting the car into total darkness. Gasps filled the subway, followed by moans of frustration as the metal bullet came to a grinding halt.

"What the hell?" the homely man growled. "I'm in no mood for this today, so they better get us back on our way, pronto."

"I told you," the elderly woman griped, echoing the upset man's displeasure for the stalled subway. "This city needs to fix what our tax payer dollars pay for."

Powerless World

Sarah looped her arm through the straps of her purse as she dug in the pocket of her pants for her phone. The last thing she wanted was to have someone try something in the dark.

A light from the opposite end of the car sliced through the ether of blackness. It waived in the air, shinning over the irritated faces of the passengers who sat in their seats.

"I don't think it's just the subway that's messed up," Sarah said while looking through the windows that lined the sides of the car. "It's just as dark out in the tunnel."

The large woman across from Sarah turned and looked in the direction they came. "She's right. It's just as dark out there. I can't see any sort of light."

Sarah got her phone out and thumbed the power button. The gleam from the screen lit up. She engaged the phone's flashlight and skimmed over the car.

The passengers peered through the windows at the darkness as they held their belongings close to their persons.

"Well, isn't this just great?" the homely man groused with a heavy sigh. He grabbed the collar of the smirched rags draped over his large frame and fanned his body. He stood from his seat and paced back and forth. He ran his hand over what few strands of hair covered his head. "There's no airflow now, so it's going to get hot as hell in here. Just how I wanted to spend my way home from work after a long night and morning of working my ass off. Sweating to death in this tin can."

"I don't see any lights anywhere, either," the stocky businessman at the end of the car called out. He peered through the windows into the next car, then said, "Looks like it's all of the cars from what I can tell."

"Holy hell," the homely man groaned.

Sarah crept to the rear of the car. The light from the phone washed over the empty seats and steel bars. Her arm pressed down on her purse. She was hesitant about the homely man, given his angered state. He made her feel uncomfortable.

Sarah leaned toward the glass and squinted, trying to look through the car behind them for any spec or hint of light within the murk.

It appeared to be empty. She didn't see any shadowy figures in the rows of seats. The small lights mounted on the interior of the tunnel walls were void of any life. They should be active.

"I think the power is out everywhere," she said aloud. "At least, in the tunnel, anyway. I don't think it's a city problem or anything like that. I think it's something bigger."

"Do you work for the city or know anything about the subway system?" the homely man snapped.

Sarah glanced over her shoulder to the homely man, then rolled her eyes. "No, I don't, but I do know that the lights on the interior of the tunnel walls should be lit. They have backup generators for when the power goes out, right? From the looks of it, they aren't working either. If they were, the tunnel should have power, at least."

"Are you sure about that?" the homely man scoffed. "Because I've never heard of that. There have been instances where subways in other states have lost power and the tunnels went dark. No lights of any kind stayed on, so your whole generator theory is flawed. Thanks for that insightful tidbit."

The man's condescending tone crawled all over Sarah. He was an ass and didn't fight to hide the fact. He wasn't helping the situation in the least.

"Excuse me, sir," the elderly woman interjected. "Do you work for the subway transit authority?"

He stumbled over his words, then rubbed the back of his head as he cut his gaze over to Sarah. "Well, no, but-"

"So, you don't know for sure, then," she countered.

He shrugged as his face swelled with embarrassment. "No. Not really."

"Okay, so keep your opinion to yourself if you're not open to others," she fired back.

He folded his arms across his chest. His face twisted into a scowl as he huffed, then looked away.

The elderly woman winked at Sarah, then gave her a half smile which was hard to see. "I'm Nancy, by the way."

"Sarah."

"Actually, most cities with subways have started installing generators for this reason. I'm not sure if Boston has yet or not, but I know New York looked into doing it," the large woman said. "I used to work for the Transit System here in Boston some years back. My name is Debbie, in case you were wondering."

"Hi, Debbie," Nancy replied.

"Oh great. Another expert," the homely man grumbled. "And can we please focus on the task at hand? I'm Tom, and you are?"

Tom pointed at the businessman in a huff. "Chris."

"There. We're all besties now. Can we get back to what really matters?" Tom snarled.

Sarah grabbed the silver handle to the passthrough door. A loud banging noise rose from the opposite end of the car. She turned on her heels and stared down the long stretch of seats and steel poles.

Chris shined his phone at the connecting door that led into the next car. He stepped cautiously toward the commotion and lifted his phone at the glass window.

A woman hammered the window with her fist. She yelled at the glass, but it was hard to make out.

Chris trained his ear to the window and listened closely, trying to discern what she was saying.

"What's going down over there?" Debbie shouted. She sprung from her seat in a blink while pointing at the frantic passenger.

"They managed to crack one of the doors, but it jammed. It won't go any farther," Chris replied. "They tried the emergency button to contact the operator, but it isn't working. They're asking if we can open any of the doors in our car or reach the operator?"

Sarah grabbed the gray handle and jerked, but it wouldn't budge. Both hands wrapped around the handle as she tugged some more, but to no avail. "It won't move."

She held her phone up and spotted a sign to the side of the door.

Not a Passthrough.

That's great. Must be locked, then.

Below the sign was the emergency call button.

Sarah pressed the small red button, then released. No static or hint of a connection could be heard. It was dead. "The emergency system isn't working in here, either."

Chris trained his phone at the automatic doors. He stepped closer and ran his hand down the seam where the two sides met. "I wonder if we can pry them open."

Debbie shook her head, then waved her plump finger in the air. "We should wait for the operator. If the subway goes offline, the transit authority will be notified, and they'll send a team down here to evacuate us from the car if the conductor cannot and if it's safe to do so."

"What sort of response time do they have in these sorts of matters if the operator can't open the doors?" Chris asked.

"Hopefully, not too long," Debbie said. "Could be fifteen minutes or a few hours. Just depends on what all is going on and if there are other cars that are stuck."

Tom squinted his eyes and shook his head while pointing at the double doors. "Hold on. Wait a minute and backup here. What do you mean if it's safe to do so?"

All of the passengers paused and stared at her. The car fell silent as each person waited for a response.

Debbie gulped. "What if this is some sort of terrorist attack, like an EMP strike or a bomb that has been set off by the North Korean's or the Islamic State? That tunnel could be filled with toxic fumes or radiation. Remember 9/11? The Boston Marathon? I'm just saying that could be it, and we should use our heads and think. Why else would ALL of the power just go out?"

Sarah listened to the bickering passengers volley their wild theories. It did little to stay the uneasiness lingering inside her head.

She didn't know why the power crashed, or what had happened. Something did, and that made Sarah hesitant to act for fear of the unknown.

For now, their best bet was to stay put and wait for help, regardless if they liked it or not.

Derek Shupert

CHAPTER SEVEN

RUSSELL

Pain lanced through every part of Russell's body as he came to. Disorientation filled his head. It hurt to move and breathe. For now, though, he was alive.

A grumble of discomfort escaped Russell's lips. His eyes were heavy as he forced them open. A thick haze coated his vision and made it hard to see. He blinked, trying to erase the film.

How long have I been out?

"Tim," Russell spoke through a groan as he tried to move. "You ok, bud?"

Nothing but the whistling of the wind answered him from the multiple breaches within the fuselage. The foul stench of smoke filled Russell's nose and made him cough. His throat burned, and his lungs stung with each hack he made.

Russell's face scrunched in pain as he lifted his hand to his head. The movement stole his breath and made him pant.

His eyes clamped shut, then opened wide.

The blurred vision waned as the battered interior of the Cessna materialized. Devastation surrounded Russell. Plumes of smoke escaped from the front of the aircraft. Jagged pieces of glass rimmed the outer edge of the windshield like sharks' teeth.

Tim hadn't responded. He was motionless. His arms hung lifeless by his sides. Blood dripped from the tips of his fingers. The side of his head rested against the headrest as he looked away from Russell.

"Come on, bud. Wake up." Russell reached over and grabbed his arm. "Now's not the time for a nap. We need to figure out where we are."

Russell tugged at Tim's arm, trying to get any sort of indicator that his friend was alive. Tim moved only in response to having his arm pulled.

A jolt of fear spiked through Russell. His lips quivered and his eyes glossed over with the realization that his friend could be dead.

Russell lifted from the seat, but the seat belt snapped to and kept him from going any further. Anger and sadness boiled in his stomach as he feared for Tim's life. Panic set in as he fumbled with the latch to set himself free.

The metal ends of the seat belt slapped against the center console and the fuselage. More pain punished Russell as he leaned toward Tim.

Tim's not dead. He's not dead, Russell muttered to himself.

He grabbed Tim's chin and pulled his head toward him. Those few seconds of not knowing felt like an eternity. His heart pounded inside his ear as Tim's bloody face came into view.

Powerless World

A wide gash ran from the top of his brow down to the other side of his chin. Russell froze. His eyes swelled with emotion as he fought to hold it together. He placed two fingers on his neck, hoping he'd discover a pulse, regardless of how faint it may be.

Russell knew it was a longshot, but he hoped against hope that Tim might still be with him. He searched, moving his fingers over Tim's moist neck, only to find that his friend had passed.

Son of a bitch.

What light at the end of the tunnel Russell had seen before they took off from the airport seemed to evaporate in a blink. His best friend was dead, and he was stranded in the wilderness without a clue of what to do next.

He wasn't a survivalist, and didn't know how to live off the land. He was a city boy through and through. He had been on some hikes as a kid, but that was about it.

Trekking through the woods with no clear direction felt like a bad move, but staying put and not doing anything wouldn't work either.

Russell didn't know what to do next. His body was riddled with pain, and his best friend was dead, but he had survived. If it were to remain that way, he had to venture into the unknown and find help.

The phone.

Russell forced his hand into the front pocket of his jeans. The cool, crisp mountain air brushed over his flesh. A shiver washed over his body as he yanked it out.

Please work. Please work.

His hands trembled as he thumbed the power button. The screen flashed and came to life. The device couldn't work fast enough for Russell as he pressed the phone icon.

In the top corner of the screen, he noticed the zero with a line through it. No signal.

Russell's shoulders sagged with defeat. A heavy sigh fled his mouth. He lifted his hand up to his face and grunted in discomfort. His shoulder hurt. Certain movements tormented him without pause. The pain stole his breath and made him weak in the knees. A possible dislocation or sprain. Either way, it hurt like hell.

The wave of pain subsided and gave Russell a reprieve. He secured the phone in the front of his pants, and gave Tim one final look. He hated to leave his friend, but he had to move.

Light bled in through the gaping hole of the fuselage as Russell left the cockpit. Wires hung from the ceiling. The long strands of cable looked like snakes dangling from trees. They swayed from side to side with the breeze.

Russell ducked and shoved them out of his way with his good arm as he traversed the disheveled mess. The two seats in the rear of the Cessna were ripped from the floor. They sat on their sides with the sharp ends of the contorted metal attached to the steel legs of the seats.

The aircraft moved and creaked a loud warning, stopping Russell dead in his tracks. His arms spanned out to the side of him which ripped a grumble of pain from his lips. The hole in the fuselage was close. It was well within his reach.

Another step forward and the busted aircraft pitched portside, sending Russell flat on his ass.

He glanced to the opening, then drew a sharp breath. The plane continued to shift and creak.

Russell stood and stumbled for the cavernous hole. The aircraft pitched further portside and lifted into the air. The razor-sharp edges of the fuselage sliced across his palm as Russell grabbed the barbed ends. The cut wasn't bad, but bled some. He pulled with all his might and leapt from the Cessna as it tumbled from the cliff.

Powerless World

The rocky face of the ground pummeled Russell. A yelp of pain slithered through his clenched teeth as he hit hard on the side of his sore shoulder. He cradled his arm and watched the plane vanish below the edge of the cliff.

Russell rolled to his back and took a moment, allowing the pain to subside. He laid there, panting and trying to control his breathing.

A thunderous crash echoed throughout the canyon. Tortured metal groaned. Not only had Russell lost his best friend, but he didn't have any gear.

No extra clothes.

No supplies of any kind.

Just the torn, bloody rags he had on and the few items he had stuffed in his pockets was all he had to brave the wild.

Russell laid there, alone and afraid. He wasn't prepared for the harrowing journey ahead. If he had any hope of making it back to civilization and Sarah, alive, he would have to go through hell to do it.

Derek Shupert

CHAPTER EIGHT

SARAH

The car had grown silent, but the tension remained.

Time passed without word from the operator, or the authorities for that matter. It had been at least an hour or more from when the subway had come to a screeching halt, and the world went dark.

The absence of light made Sarah feel vulnerable. The Creeper wouldn't leave her thoughts, no matter how hard she tried to force him out. Her skin crawled from thinking about him.

The passengers grew restless, pacing about the murk to alleviate the stress that gnawed at them. Heavy sighs and footfalls rattled inside Sarah's head. The stagnant flow of air made things worse.

Sarah sat in the corner seat toward the rear of the car. Her head rested against the window as she stared out into the nothingness, wondering what had happened on the surface. The ground above them had trembled and quaked.

Did a bomb explode from a terrorist plot? If so, a small part of Sarah hoped that the fallout took out the Creeper, and she'd be free of him.

"This is bullshit," Tom groused. "They're not coming to rescue us because something horrible happened up there. I know I'm not the only one who felt the ground shake earlier. That sounded like an explosion of some kind." He stood in the middle of the car, with only the vague outline of his body visible.

Sarah's eyesight had grown accustomed to the dark, allowing her to see the other passengers as shadowy figures that moved within the ether. Cell phones were kept off to conserve battery life.

"They'll—come," Debbie breathed heavily. "We just have to be—patient, and wait a little longer—is all. We still don't know if it's safe out there."

Tom snapped at her with a hoarse growl. "Yeah, we know what your plan is; sit in this steel coffin and wait to die. Got it. It's not like we haven't been doing that for the last few hours or so. If they haven't shown up yet, I doubt they're coming to help." He pointed at each of the passengers and continued, "Whether any one of you wants to admit it, we're on our own here. We need some air flow moving through here, which means we're going to need to make some tough decisions. They're still kicking over there, even with their door being cracked open, so that at least says we should be good."

A bright light, from Chris's phone, cut through the darkness and washed over the passengers' flushed, moist faces. His striped dress shirt clung to his chest, soaked in sweat.

"If that time comes, we'll make that decision as a group. No one put you in charge, friend," he barked.

Powerless World

Tom peered at him, his body stern and rigid. His chest bowed, like a gorilla being challenged by a rival male. "First off, I'm not your friend. Second, someone needs to step up here and take charge, or we're all going to die. If the rest of you want to, that's your bit, but I'm not sucking in my last breath in this damn coffin."

Sarah stood from her seat in a flash with the back of her phone facing the heated men. Light shone from the device as she raised her hands in the air. The squabble needed to be squashed and dealt with by a rational person.

"I think we need to calm down before matters get out of hand." Sarah felt like she was talking to a couple of kids who were having a spat over a toy. It seemed ridiculous, and yet, considering how Tom had been acting, felt like it was par for the course. "Arguing and fighting isn't going to solve anything, or help us figure out what to do next. We're all frustrated, and want to get out of here, but losing our cool isn't going to accomplish that."

Tom peered over his shoulder at Sarah. The scowl on his face grew deeper, his furrowed brow more rigid as he balled his fingers into fists.

He didn't like being scorned in such a manner, that much was apparent. Between Nancy, Chris, and now Sarah, he had reached the end of his rope.

Tom pointed at Sarah. "Listen, no one was talking to you, so why don't you sit your happy ass down, and let the men handle business, all right?"

The degrading remark shocked Sarah. She had never been talked to in such manner, and wasn't going to allow it to go any further. "I'll do just that once you stop acting like a five-year-old."

His nostrils flared as he took a step toward Sarah.

She grabbed the latch on her purse, her hands trembling. She wanted her Glock. It was the one thing that made her feel safe in the moment.

Chris stomped across the car and reached for Tom's arm. He grabbed a handful of the smirched rags and pulled. "That's enough of that."

Anger swelled in Tom's dingy face. He spun on his heels and elbowed Chris in the nose. He stumbled backward into a chair, but didn't go down.

The businessman stormed the mentally unstable tyrant and speared him in the mid-section with his shoulder. The men grappled for control as they drew closer to Sarah. She grabbed the grip of the Glock as the brawling brutes slammed into her, knocking the purse and Glock to the floor.

Both the purse and Glock clattered off the steel which caused both men to halt their engagement.

Sarah had the light trained at the ground while searching for her piece. It came into view as Tom spotted it as well. He looked to Sarah, then back to the weapon.

He kneed Chris in the gut, then rammed his elbow in his spine. Tom threw the businessman against the row of seats and went for the Glock.

Sarah beat him by a mere second and scooped up the Glock. She backed away, then chambered a rounded.

She trained the weapon at Tom's chest. "Cool it now, and sit your ass down, or I will shoot you."

Tom raised his hands in a placating gesture. A wiry grin slit across his sweaty face. He sized Sarah up. "I don't think you have the balls to pull that trigger."

The Glock remained fixed on Tom's torso. Sarah didn't want to shoot him, but she had to protect herself, and the other passengers, from his choleric state of mind. She hoped he'd heed her warning, and not push her any further. "I guarantee my balls are bigger than yours. Don't force my hand unless you want to find out how big they are."

The man's tongue slithered out of his mouth and over his chapped lips. The wiry grin remained.

Debbie didn't say a word as she aided the battered businessman to his feet.

Tom tilted his head, acknowledging the threat as his arms lowered. Sarah kept both hands on the grip and followed suit while watching his every move.

The homely man's elbows touched his sides, and he lunged forward.

The Glock barked.

White flashed from the muzzle.

Sarah's phone dropped to the floor, screen down.

A single round tore through Tom's chest at point blank range. His face twisted into a mask of shock as he stumbled backward.

The tips of his fingers probed the hole. His legs went limp, and he fell to the ground. Shallow breaths escaped his mouth as he looked at her with wide eyes.

He had forced her hand, and paid for that mistake with his life.

CHAPTER NINE

RUSSELL

The dense, rich vegetation of the Blue Ridge Mountains seemed endless, a vast spread of lush, vibrant green that spanned as far as the eye could see. Sprawling oak trees and cove forests coated the lands, and Russell was lost somewhere in the thick of it all.

The forest floor was carpeted with broken limbs from the surrounding trees and portions of the aircraft. The mixture of small and large branches crunched under Russell's boots as he stepped around the remains of the plane.

Russell's gaze flitted to the cloudy sky. The canopy had been shredded by the Cessna plowing through its umbrella. Jagged ends from the broken limbs looked like spears pointing at the heavens. Any branches that remained intact were void of any leaves.

Powerless World

The spike of adrenaline waned, and the scope of damage done became all too real. His shoulder throbbed, among other parts of his body.

A stabbing pain festered in Russell's side. His head pounded like a snare drum with each step he took. His ankle radiated trouble when he applied pressured. It hurt to breathe, but that could've been because of the plane crash.

What a day it had already been, and it was only going to get worse from there.

Russell licked his parched lips. He craved something wet and it wasn't water. A stiff drink on the rocks crossed his mind. He needed to take the edge off and dull the pain. It didn't matter what poison filled his belly. Jack Daniels or Wild Turkey. Any would do. Beggars couldn't be choosers.

In times of extreme stress, Russell bowed to the spirits. Deep down, he didn't want to be their slave, but his will was weak, and he struggled to resist the urge. He planned to fight that bond, and break free. Whatever it took to get Sarah back, he was willing to work his hardest to make that happen.

Russell stopped and took a moment to catch his breath. His shoulders sagged with exhaustion as he bent over. The palm of his hand pressed to the rigid surface of the tree he stood next to while the heel of his other hand jammed into the soft part just above his knee.

Each step he had taken was laborious at best, and it wasn't getting any better. He had been slogging through the dense verdure for what seemed like forever, but he hadn't traveled too far.

The plane wreck lingered in his head. It was difficult to comprehend and felt unreal. He'd survived the crash, but his best friend was dead.

What the hell happened, anyway?

It was a question that wouldn't leave his thoughts. He tried to figure out the cause, but came up empty. A short in the engine? Possible. But that didn't explain the aircraft's loss of communication and the navigation going haywire beforehand.

Russell rubbed his eyes, then blinked. A heavy sigh spewed from his lips as he skimmed over the foliage that surrounded him.

The forest looked the same, regardless of where Russell went. He couldn't tell if he was heading for civilization or further away into the unknown. That did little to calm his frayed nerves.

Before moving on, Russell turned and leaned into the tree, then dug his hand into the pockets of his jeans. He pulled out the contents. There wasn't much.

A couple packs of peppermint gum, to help curb the urge for a drink, his cell phone, and a lighter that Tim had asked him to hold onto. Even though Russell also smoked at times, he felt it had only to be fair that he'd given Tim hell about his bad habit since he did the same for his drinking.

They had each agreed to keep the other in check as much as possible, which proved to be futile in the end.

The one thing that Russell missed the most was his silver flask. He had told himself to leave it, and that he was strong enough to go without. At that moment, alone and hurt in the woods, with his best friend dead, and no help in sight, he regretted his decision.

The inside of Russell's mouth felt arid. His gums were tacky to the touch. Although his body craved a stiff drink, he knew he needed some water to keep from getting dehydrated.

Russell pulled a stick of gum from the pack and removed the foil. He shoved the gum into his mouth and chewed. The items clutched in his hands were secured back into his pockets as he plotted out his next move.

Powerless World

Sweat and trickles of blood raced down the sides of his face. The sleeve of his tattered wind breaker swiped across his forehead as he looked over the lush environment.

Birds squawked overhead.

Animals rustled within the bushes around him.

There wasn't much of a path to follow. It didn't look like people ventured this way often, if ever. Any grass stood unchallenged, and there weren't any footprints within the foliage.

It was a best guess scenario that faced him on which way to go. Standing around wasn't going to get him home, or the medical attention that he knew he needed. Survive or die was the name of the game, and he had no choice but to play.

Russell pushed away from the tree and stumbled down through the narrow opening that wound through a thicket of bushes.

The terrain pitched at a steep angle. Rocks littered the soil and added a degree of difficulty to navigate it safely.

The soles of his boots slipped over the surface of the rocks as Russell leaned back. He grunted and grimaced through the pain as his good arm pressed to the ground.

Slow and steady, he maneuvered down the slope until he reached the bottom. His ankle gave and sent him tumbling the rest of the way.

The bed of uneven earth and large, thick tree roots broke his fall. The side of his head bounced off the ground. His face contorted as he cussed under his breath.

Russell lifted from the ground and shook his head. He rested on his knees while gripping his injured shoulder. Dirt clung to the sweat and splotches of blood that ran down from his hairline.

The snapping of branches close by caught his attention. His eyes went wide, and his head swiveled as he searched for the source.

It didn't sound like a small animal. The noise was too loud for that. It had to be something larger. Perhaps a person?

"Hello. Is anyone there?" His voice was raspy. He struggled to get his wobbly legs under him.

No response was given, but the rustling remained. It climbed in volume with each second that passed. A cold chill washed over Russell as he turned in a circle, looking for the source. He couldn't find what was lurking within the dense verdure, but he knew something was there.

Panic set in.

Naked fear took over.

Russell's heart punched his chest. The stinging prick of fright surged through his veins. He was being stalked by something, but couldn't see what it was.

A predator had no doubt gotten wind of his scent. He was an injured animal ripe for the picking.

A low growl loomed from the bushes and snatched the voice from Russell's throat. He gulped, then backed away. Snapshots of the animal's solid, tawny color bled through the thicket. It sounded like a cat of some sort.

Russell kept his gaze fixed on the bushes as he moved away. The puma stalked to the edge of the brush, then stopped shy of breaching the small clearing.

The fronts of its large paws pressed into the ground as it lowered its head. It's golden-yellow eyes honed in on Russell.

Fight or flight. It was as simple as that.

Russell had no qualms about his ability to defend himself, but he had never been faced with a predator that had sharp claws and teeth and hunger for fresh meat.

The puma growled louder. Its body stayed close to the ground as it moved out from the bushes.

Powerless World

Russell turned, then ran in the opposite direction. Pain stabbed his ankle as he forced his way through the vegetation. Branches snapped. The pointed ends punched his stomach and torso. His arms were up in front of him to shield his face as he fought to put as much distance between him and the wild animal as possible.

The puma sprinted after its meal. The footfalls of the large cat pounded close behind him, but Russell couldn't lay eyes on the animal.

Fear swallowed him whole, and kept his legs moving at a good clip. Pain was a byproduct of the horror that chased after him.

Russell emerged from the thicket that opened up into a small plot of open land. Swaths of tall oak trees lined the periphery, among other rich greenery. He could hear what sounded like running water. A stream?

He peered over his shoulder, and spotted the puma racing toward him. The cat's gaze wouldn't deviate from Russell. It was locked in and wasn't going to stop until it overtook him.

The swollen ankle grew more agitated. The pulsating made it hard to maintain a brisk pace. He couldn't keep it going for much longer.

The edge of the stream came into view. If he could just get across, then maybe he'd have a chance, and the large cat would discontinue its pursuit.

The puma swatted his legs. Russell lost his balance and tumbled into the chilled water. His head dipped below the surface for a split second before emerging. Another big splash landed next to him as he paddled to the other side.

Water spat from his mouth as he focused on the dry land. His one good arm propelled him forward as fast as it could.

The tips of Russell's fingers dug into the mud. He pulled with every ounce of strength he had left in his body. His legs kicked, splashing water in every direction.

Soaked to the bone, his clothes clung to his battered frame. He climbed the small embankment and crested the edge. He spotted the wet, tawny fur of the puma as the creature splashed through the water toward him.

Russell swung at the animal in a feeble attempt to keep the predator at bay. The puma went for his throat, but latched onto his forearm. Its sharp fangs punctured the skin.

"Awww," he cried out as the animal pulled and thrashed its head.

Pain stole Russell's voice as the animal dragged his body onto even ground. Intense pressure clamped over his arm like a vise. He tried to pull it free from the puma's mouth, but it wouldn't budge.

Bark. Bark.

What is that? Russell thought. A dog?

The puma stopped, then lifted its head. Russell reeled in his arm as the cat's ears twitched and searched for the source.

Lying prone on his stomach, Russell remained still, motionless. He shivered from being wet, but also from being scared to death. His life flashed before his eyes, and the thought of never seeing Sarah again tormented him. Hopefully, whatever distracted the large cat would draw it away, and leave him be.

A blur of dark brown fur with black mixed in broke from the tall grass behind the puma. The cat hissed and lowered down as the animal approached.

Russell closed his eyes and covered his head. Heavy breaths pushed from his mouth as he listened to the animals fight. Growling and barking swarmed him as dirt was kicked over him.

The report from a rifle crackled in the air. Russell jolted. He removed his arm and lifted his face.

Powerless World

The strife among the opposing animals ended. The large cat hissed, then scampered away. Its tawny fur vanished within the brush. The legs of the dog stood near him. Its panted breath played in Russell's ear.

"Max," a soft but worried feminine voice called out. "You all right, boy?"

Bark.

A person. Thank, God.

Russell flopped over to his side, then flat on his back. The sun shone through the puffy white clouds which caused him to blink and close his weary eyes.

The footsteps hammered the ground as the dog groaned. It sniffed Russell's body, then licked his face.

"What have I told you, Max, about-" She came to a grinding halt. "Oh. So that's why you took off." Russell could see her legs and the thick-soled boots she wore, but that was all. His head tilted to the side as his trembling arm shielded the sky from his view.

"Come here, Max," she called.

The dog sniffed a bit more, but obeyed her command. She knelt next to Russell. The butt plate of her rifle rested on the ground. She glanced over Russell's body as Max sat on his haunches beside her.

"Dear lord, are you ok?"

Russell lowered his arm to the ground as she hovered over him. Her head blotted out the sun and illuminated her golden blonde hair that tickled his nose and cheeks. It made her look almost angelic. Her face scrunched in worry as she stared into his shiny eyes.

"Please, help me."

CHAPTER TEN

SARAH

N umb to the touch. That's how Sarah felt as she towered over the dying man. A look of disbelief flooded her face. She felt detached, as if the moment wasn't real, but instead, some messed up dream.

Did I just kill him? Christ. What have I done?

She had fired the Glock 43 numerous times at paper targets and wooden boards. She had shattered glass bottles and punctured tin cans, but Sarah had never shot anyone before.

Tom gasped his last breath. His arms fell lifeless to his sides. Blood pooled under his body, and spread out in a circle. She secured the Glock between her waistband and knelt down beside him.

"Is he—dead?" Debbie whimpered.

Chris trained his flashlight at the deceased man's face. His eyes were open, mouth agape.

Powerless World

Sarah reached over his body and checked his neck for a pulse. Her fingers pressed to Tom's clammy skin, checking his carotid artery for a heartbeat. She hoped against hope that he might still be alive, but would it matter? The hole in his chest looked fatal, and they hadn't seen or heard from the operator or Transit Authority. It felt as though they were alone, and left to their own devices.

Nothing.

Not even a hint at life.

She bowed her head, then closed his eyes with her fingertips.

"Oh, Christ," Debbie sputtered. Tears streamed down her face.

Sarah sat on her backside while staring at the body. Guilt racked her through and through. The man was a dick, and she felt justified in what she did, but that didn't make it any easier. Taking a person's life was an experience she thought she'd never have to face. She hated him for forcing her hand. It didn't have to go down as it had.

Chris glanced at Sarah. Blood trickled down the crease from the side of his busted lip. "You didn't have a choice. He was out of control, and our lives were in danger. You did the right thing. We all saw it."

Perhaps, but it didn't soften the blow of killing an unarmed man.

The steel walls of the subway car closed in around Sarah. It stifled her breathing. She felt trapped, and needed some space to process what had happened.

Sarah grabbed her phone, then stood from the floor. She paced about for a few moments, struggling to come to terms with her actions.

Debbie leaned forward. She craned her neck, then pointed at the elderly woman who was lying on her side. "Has anyone checked on Nancy recently?"

Sarah had forgotten about the woman and hadn't thought to check on her. She had grown silent some time back, and she figured she just fell asleep.

"Ma'am, are you ok?" Sarah asked while reaching out to the motionless woman. Her voice was unsteady and cracked. Trepidation consumed her hand as she tapped the woman's arm.

The elderly woman faced the backs of the seats. Sarah couldn't get a good look at her face. She didn't respond or move, which made Sarah fear the worst.

"She's not dead, also, is she?" Debbie cringed.

Sarah grabbed Nancy's arm and pulled. Her body tilted toward the floor with no resistance. She shined the light from her phone over the old woman's aged face.

Her eyes were sealed, mouth clamped shut. The cane sat nestled next to her.

Sarah probed her neck for a pulse, but found none. "She's gone as well."

Debbie gasped, then stood from her seat. "Oh my God."

Lights from the other car shone through the fogged-up windows. They moved like lasers, slicing through the murk.

Sarah moved the woman back the way she was, then stepped away.

Chris stood at her side and peered at the body. "I don't think help is coming anytime soon. We need to consider busting out of here any way we can." His gaze dipped to her waist at the Glock she had stashed away.

He was right. They had to do something. Hanging inside the car was no longer an option. They had to find their way to the surface on their own.

Sarah bowed in agreement, then turned toward the emergency exit at the rear of the car.

She retrieved the Glock from her waistband and walked to the sealed door. The weapon sat tight in her grip. Her fingers repositioned as she shined the light at the lock below the handle.

The Glock trembled in her hand which made it difficult to hone in on the target. A deep breath filled Sarah's lungs as she fought to stay the jitters of discharging the weapon.

Her finger slipped over the trigger as she steadied her arm. Just five pounds of pressure is all it took to fire another round.

Sarah tugged on the trigger.

The Glock barked.

She flinched.

Fire spat from the barrel.

A single round struck the lock on the door, damaging the device.

Sarah lowered the weapon to her side and stepped toward the door. She placed the Glock in her waistband and grabbed the handle. Footfalls from the steel floor played in her head. Both Debbie and Chris flanked her.

She wrenched the door open. The stagnant air from the tunnel flowed into the car.

Sarah breathed in. It felt good to be free of the confines of the car. Her nose didn't detect any sort of chemical or other substance, although, radiation wasn't something one could smell. Still, it was a risk that had to be taken.

"Well?" Debbie asked. "Is it safe?"

Sarah shrugged. She didn't know for sure if it was or not. "Don't know, but I'm not smelling anything out of the ordinary."

The light from her phone dipped to the clamp that held the car in front of her in place. She tilted the device to the side in the direction of the ether that seemed hollow and endless. It only penetrated so far which didn't offer her anymore of an idea as to what happened.

Sarah skirted the narrow walkway to the edge of the car. She hopped down to the ground below. The dull thud of her weight landing echoed through the tunnel.

"I'm going to check on the operator. See if I can figure out what the hell is going on here," Sarah advised.

Debbie and Chris emerged from the car with his flashlight engaged. They moved along the walkway, following Sarah as she proceeded onward.

It was odd being in such a place with no ambient light of any sort. Anytime Sarah had ridden the subway, when she glanced out of the windows, she could see the amber glow from the mounted lights along the walls. It didn't make the tunnel feel so vast and empty.

Beams of light shone through the windows of the other cars. They moved, and shifted as they tilted to the ground, trying to see what was going on.

Sarah kept her free hand on the grip of the Glock as she walked past the cars. She looked to the foggy windows above at the passengers that swiped their palms over the glass to get a better look.

Chris and Debbie followed her, but only at a distance. Within the eerie silence, Sarah could hear the woman whimpering at any sort of sound that crept up. She knew how she felt. Sarah was just as afraid. As she had learned with the Creeper, one had to face those things that scared one most, and push on, despite the fear.

The passengers hammered the windows with their fists, trying to get her attention. Any words spoken were difficult, if not impossible, to discern. Sarah motioned with her hand for them to stay put.

Powerless World

Sarah approached the front of the subway where the operator should be. No light of any sort shone from the windows of the car which made her feel uneasy. Her hands shook and her pulse spiked. A lump of fear formed in her throat as she forced it down. She turned and swept the tunnel with her phone while trying to remain calm and collected.

"Hello?" she called up to the cab of the car. "Is anyone there?"

Sarah craned her neck and took a step back toward the railing behind her. She lifted the phone high in the air while standing on the tips of her toes, trying to get a better look. From where she stood, Sarah couldn't lay eyes on the operator.

A set of steps built into the frame of the car caught her attention. She approached the car and grabbed the railings on both sides. Slow and steady, she scaled the side to the small platform.

Sarah leaned forward and narrowed her gaze through the window as she waived the phone like a wand. Inside, she spotted a body slumped over the control board of the car. She hammered the thick pane window, trying to get his attention.

"Hey," she yelled. "Are you ok?"

The operator didn't move. His body was motionless, much like the elderly woman who had passed. The blue cap he wore was jerked to the side and concealed his face. Both arms rested on the control board. Not a single twitch or hint of life showed from his hands. He did have something clutched within his fingers, but she couldn't make it out.

Sarah moved around the platform of the front of the car. She positioned herself at the door that led into the cab, but was still unable to obtain a clear view of the operator's face. Dangling from his hip, she noticed a set of silver keys.

The door was locked, but that didn't surprise her. She figured it would be since it's where the controls for the subway were. She pounded her fist against the window one last time, hoping to snare his attention before she took matters into her own hands.

He didn't respond.

Sarah pulled the Glock from her waistband, then stepped away from the door. She moved to the side and brought the pistol to bear at the window. She squeezed the trigger and fired a single round. The glass shattered.

The sharp report echoed through the hollow tunnel. Footsteps pummeled the ground toward her. Then Debbie and Chris materialized from the murk.

"What happened?"

Sarah tilted the phone down at the inside of the door. "There's something wrong with the operator. He's slumped over the control board and doesn't appear to be responsive."

She tucked the Glock under her arm, then reached inside the cab of the car. Her fingers fiddled with the lock until it slid free.

Sarah grabbed the silver handle and jerked the door open. The operator remained stiff and motionless. She grabbed the dark blue hat and lifted it from his head.

His brown hair was damp and thick with moisture. Sweat populated his brow and coated the rest of his face. His eyes were agape, mouth slit apart. She trained the light at his hand and leaned forward.

A blue device with a silver tip rested within his grasp. Sarah gripped the top and worked it free of his hold. It was an inhaler from what she could tell.

Sarah shook the device. It felt empty, spent. She checked for a pulse on his wrist. He had none. Another dead body to add to the others.

Powerless World

Death loomed large over the subway, and was plucking the passengers at will.

The operator's body covered most of the control board, which combined with the darkness, made it that much harder to tell where everything was located.

Her hands pressed to the side of the dash as Sarah craned her neck. On the other side of the body was a radio. She reached over and grabbed the receiver. She thumbed the button on the side.

"Is anyone there? The subway heading to Copley Station has lost power with passengers aboard. We've been stranded for two hours or more."

Silence filled the line. No static or hint of a connection was heard.

Sarah dropped the receiver and sighed. Help wasn't coming, at least, not anytime soon.

The keys to open the subway car doors. They needed those.

Sarah retrieved the silver metal loop from the operator's waist and left the cab. She thumbed through the keys, unsure which one would unlock the other cars on the subway.

"The operator is dead, and the radio isn't working," Sarah said. "Not sure what happened to him, but it could've been because of the empty inhaler I found in his hand."

Debbie took a step back while Chris offered her his hand. Sarah took his hand and made her way down the side of the car. She dropped to the ground and turned to face them.

"I got these keys off the operator's belt. I'd imagine one of them is going to open the doors to the cars."

Chris took the keys from Sarah. "I'll see if I can figure out which ones work, and get the passengers out." He turned and headed for the next car.

Debbie folded her arms across her chest. Her face was flushed, eyes filled with tears that streamed down her plump cheeks.

Sarah turned and stared down the long stretch of tunnel, wondering how far an exit might be. "Wait here and help him get the other passengers out of the car."

A look of confusion washed over Debbie's face. Her brow crinkled, and she narrowed her gaze. "Are you leaving?"

"I'm going to find a way out of here."

Powerless World

CHAPTER ELEVEN

RUSSELL

Russell drifted in and out of consciousness. Heavy panting filled his ears. The smell of an animal tingled his nose. A foul scent brushed over his face which made his stomach churn. Something sticky and moist licked his hand, then up his arm.

"Max. Leave him be, will ya?" the familiar, soft feminine voice ordered. "The last thing that poor man wants or needs is you panting in his face and licking him right now."

Max groaned, then trotted away.

Russell couldn't see the dog because of the bright light shining in his face, but he heard him gallop off through the thick brush around them. Russell was prone on his back with his body tilted at an angle. His head shifted from side to side, but not from his doing. He was being moved, dragged through the uneven terrain of the mountainous hills.

Powerless World

The dense canopy of trees overhead blotted out the sky, granting him a reprieve from the strident rays that pelted his face.

Russell blinked, dipped his chin, then opened his eyes. A tall, slender body stood in front of him, dragging him on a makeshift gurney she had made out of thick branches and a dark, green tarp. Her blonde hair had been pulled back into a ponytail. A large, green camo rucksack was strapped to her back, and a rifle hung from her shoulder.

She glanced back to Russell and dipped her chin. "Shouldn't be too much longer before we get to my cabin. We'll get you dressed properly there and warmed up."

The tattered clothes Russell wore were damp and clung to his shivering frame. His teeth chattered. The wind bit at his exposed flesh.

His arm had been wrapped with a bandana. Blood soaked through the moist, yellow fabric. The wound pulsated, and hurt like hell, much like the rest of his body.

Russell licked his coarse, sticky lips and swallowed. His stomach growled and begged for food. He was in dire shape, but yet, he had survived. He kept his mouth shut and closed his eyes.

The rest of the trek through the mountainside cut through winding paths and steep inclines. Although it wasn't the smoothest journey, it went without fault. His mysterious savior, and her brave German shepherd, Max, seemed to know the Blue Ridge Mountains through and through. There was no hesitation or doubt on where to go. They navigated the winding trails without fault.

Russell laid on the gurney, limp and motionless. He thought of Sarah and Jess, and the life they'd had. Those were some of the best times he had ever known. It wasn't always perfect, but they had love, which kept them bound together. He hated how his world flipped upside down that fateful day a year ago, when the happy life he'd carved out was ripped away from him.

Even in his dreams, it still pissed him off. Dealing with such loss never went away. One just had to deal with it the best they could and move on. That was what Russell had been struggling to do, and why Sarah drifted away from him.

Now was the time to make things right, if it wasn't too late.

The smell of food cooking filled his nose. A tantalizing scent snapped him from his slumber. Spices permeated the space around him which made his stomach grumble.

The grogginess waned as Russell cracked open his eyes. The slight film blotting his vision dissolved. Long, light brown wooden logs filled his gaze.

Where am I?

Russell was no longer moving, or being dragged across the ground. That was the last thing he remembered. He wasn't cold anymore. The chill he'd battled had left. His skin was dry, and free of moisture.

His fingers traced over the brown blanket he had draped over his body. The soft, plush mattress felt comforting against his body. It was better than the tarp or the ground by a mile.

Russell glanced around the tiny bedroom with a weary gaze. He skimmed over the light-brown textured, wooden log walls and sparse furnishings that sat in the corners of the room.

A dark oak, four-drawer chest of drawers and a rocking chair resided against the far wall. Next to the bed was a tray with wet, bloody rags and a white ceramic bowl that sat on the bedstand. Bandages and other medical tools rested on top of the scarred nightstand.

The door to the bedroom was open. Russell could see out into the kitchen. Steam rose from the pot of boiling food that brought him out of his slumber. He couldn't spot the woman who had helped him or her dog.

"Hello?" he asked in a groggy, raspy voice.

Russell listened for a response, but didn't receive one.

He sat up in the bed and leaned against the headboard. His body was stiff, but the pain had lessened. His bones ached and muscles throbbed, but it was bearable.

The covers slid off his bare chest which made him pause. He grabbed the top of the sheets and lifted them up. His body had been stripped clean of the damp rags. Even his underwear was gone.

Russell squinted his eyes and scrunched his brow as a twinge of pain pierced his temple. He dropped the covers and pressed the ends of his thumbs against the side of his head to ease the discomfort.

His arm didn't hurt as bad when he lifted it up.

A grumble slipped from his lips. With each pump of blood that coursed through his veins, his head throbbed in unison.

Footfalls creaked over the wooden floor of the cabin and headed for the bedroom. Russell released a deep breath as the woman entered the room.

She leaned against the jamb of the doorway while wiping her damp hands off on a towel. "How are you feeling? Better, I hope."

Russell licked his lips, then removed his thumbs from his temples. "I'm doing all right, thanks to you. I'm still sore, and I've got a headache, but otherwise, not bad."

She slung the towel over her shoulder, then folded her arms across her chest. A warm smile slit across her ageless face. She didn't have any make-up on, but she didn't need any. She had a natural beauty.

"That's good to hear. I fixed you up as best I could. I gave you some pain killers earlier when you were semi-awake, so that should keep the discomfort at a tolerable level. That was challenging, but you swallowed them without any issue. Your arm was dislocated, so I popped it back into place."

Russell nodded, then offered a grateful smile. "I appreciate that, and your kindness. If you hadn't come along, that mountain lion would've torn me to shreds."

The woman turned and peered back toward the kitchen. She craned her neck in the direction of the pot of food she had going. "It was Max who found you. He caught the scent and took off. I had a hard time keeping up with him."

Max trotted in from the kitchen and brushed by her side. The tips of his ears and his tail were only visible above the edge of the mattress. He skirted around the bedframe and hopped up on the side of the bed.

His tongue dangled out of his mouth with his front paws resting on the covers near Russell's legs. He leaned in close and sniffed at him, flicking his tongue out to try and lick his face.

"Seems as though Max likes you," the woman observed. "Most times, he's standoffish with guys. That, and he's pretty protective of me."

Max leaned down and nudged Russell's hand with his snout.

"I'm glad he does. If he didn't, I'd imagine I would've died out there." Russell rubbed Max's head. He massaged his crown with the tips of his fingers. He hadn't been that close to a dog for many years. Not since his deceased daughter's beagle had passed when she was twelve.

The woman patted her leg, then said, "All right, Max. That's enough for now. I imagine you'll get some more attention later."

Max licked Russell's hand one last time, then moved off the side of the bed. He trotted over to the woman's side and sat on his haunches. He was well trained and obeyed without question.

Powerless World

Russell glanced around the room for his clothes. He didn't see them on the dresser or the rocking chair. He felt a bit exposed even with the sheets and blankets covering his naked body. He hadn't been around a beautiful woman while he was naked for some time. Not since Sarah.

"What did you do with my clothes and belongings?"

The woman pointed at the nightstand. "Your phone and other personal items are in the top drawer. As far as your clothes go, I tossed them out. They were in bad shape. Torn and ripped. Plus, they were spotted with blood. Didn't think you'd want to wear such tattered rags. I've got some men's clothes that I think will fit you. I'll go grab them shortly and bring 'em to you. You're more than welcome to take what you need."

Russell turned and reached for the nightstand. He opened the drawer and found his phone and the other items he had crammed into his pocket. "Thanks. I'll take whatever you can spare. I don't have much of a choice since I'm sitting here stark naked."

The woman smirked, then blushed some as she pushed away from the jamb. "Let me go grab those clothes for you. I'll be right back."

She stepped toward the door.

"I'm Russell Cage, by the way."

The woman stopped, then said, "Nice to meet you, Russell Cage. I'm Cathy Snider."

CHAPTER TWELVE

RUSSELL

Russell gave a grateful nod as Cathy left his sight with Max by her side. He retrieved his phone from the drawer and thumbed the power button. It didn't respond to his command. The screen had streaks of moisture coating the glass. Russell rubbed the blanket over the screen and thumbed the button again.

Cathy was only gone for ten minutes or so before returning with two boxes stacked in her arms. She wobbled through the doorway and sat the cartons in the rocking chair. "There's plenty in there to choose from. Everything from regular shirts to flannel tops. The nights up here, and even days, can get a bit chilly, so I'd advise picking out some to keep you comfortable and warm."

Russell tossed his phone to the bed with a disgruntled sigh. "I appreciate it."

Cathy made for the door. She grabbed the brass doorknob, then looked at Russell. "Why don't you get dressed? The chow I've got cooking should be done. Some food might do you some good."

Russell nodded as Cathy stepped out of the room and closed the door behind her. He rubbed his hand over his face, then tossed the covers from his bare body.

The warmth that had accumulated under the layers of sheets evaporated in a blink. It wasn't too cold in the bedroom, but it wasn't near as warm as being under the covers.

Russell scooted to the edge of the bed and threw his legs to the wooden floor. The rough surface of the planks pricked the soles of his feet, and gave him pause. Russell's hands pressed down on the mattress as he stood up.

A slight twinge shot through his ankle with the pressure. It hurt some, but not as bad as it had. The room spun and made him feel off balance—a slight dizzy spell that would hopefully wane.

Russell stalked toward the boxes of clothes as the floor creaked under him. The damaged and wrinkled cardboard cartons looked aged, as if they had been sitting for some time. Russell grabbed both and moved them to the bed.

The tape on the boxes had lost its adhesion. It lifted from the dusty cardboard in places. Russell removed the tape from the tops of both, then opened the lids.

Cathy wasn't joking about an assortment. Each box was stuffed to the gills with an array of garb. Graphic tees, jeans, flannel, long-sleeve shirts, footwear, and jackets rounded out the selection.

Russell sifted through the attire, pulling out those items he wanted to try on. She had some boxers crammed in with the items. He wasn't keen on wearing another man's underwear, but considering he didn't have any, he'd have to make do.

Max barked, then groaned from the other room while Russell got dressed. The boxers, socks, jeans, shirt, and flannel top all fit without any real issues. Russell plopped down on the side of the bed and slipped on the thick-soled hiking boots. They were a tad bit larger than he normally wore, but they worked just the same. Given his swollen ankle, it made it easier to get the boot on.

Russell discarded the cartons on the floor, then shoved them against the wall. He didn't grab a jacket. The layers of shirts he had on kept him warm enough.

He grabbed the phone from the mattress and made his way around the bed to the nightstand. He retrieved the gum and lighter and stuffed them into his pockets.

The packages of gum felt damp, but Russell didn't want to trash them yet. He was craving a drink, and the gum was his only source to battle the desire.

Russell closed the drawer and made for the door. He caught a glimpse of his reflection in the oval mirror that sat on top of the chest of drawers and leaned against the log wall.

His fingers traced over the cuts and the black eye he had. He tilted his head to the side, then lowered his chin.

He looked like hell, but that was to be expected. Afterall, he had been in a plane crash and was attacked by a mountain lion. Given what happened, Russell didn't mind the surly look or the tiny lacerations that covered his stubble-ridden face. At least he was alive.

"Soup's on," Cathy called out from the kitchen. "Best to get it while it's hot."

Russell dropped his hand from his face. He tossed open the door and walked with a bit of a limp across the cabin.

He glanced over the open space that was one large room. Next to the kitchen was a grand fireplace that had a fire going. He could feel the warmth from the glow of the orange flames brush over his face.

A couch and chair were positioned in the middle of the living room with a spacious dog bed with white bones on the brown fabric between the furniture. An area rug covered the planks of wood and pushed toward the front door.

Two other rooms were against the far wall. A ladder sat positioned between both and led to a loft type area. One thing that Russell noticed was that there wasn't any sort of electronics. No TV, microwave, or anything else of the sort.

Cathy sidled up to the small round table. She had dished out two bowls of piping hot stew. Steam lifted from the food, teasing Russell's stomach. Max sat on the floor by her side and devoured the chunks of meat from his dog dish.

"Looks like you found some threads that fit," she said. "Glad I found a use for those clothes. I've been meaning to give them away. They were my late husband's clothes. Procrastination at its best, I guess."

Russell tugged at the unbuttoned flannel shirt and the jeans he had on. "Yeah. I'm glad you didn't either. This would've been a bit more awkward if you had."

Cathy chuckled while spooning out a hefty portion of stew from her blue ceramic bowl. She blew over the food before taking a bite. "I hope you like the food. It has deer meat in it with an assortment of veggies. Corn, green beans, potatoes, and carrots."

Russell pulled the aged wooden chair away from the table and took a seat. He grabbed the spoon and probed the stew. The rich scent of spices made his mouth water.

"It smells delicious," he said while taking a bite. The torrid stew rolled about his mouth until it cooled some, then slipped down his throat. "Haven't had stew in I don't know how long."

Cathy took another generous bite before responding. "Thanks. I keep it pretty simple, and fix whatever is easiest on the stove top."

Russell gulped down another portion of the medley. Juices ran down his chin. He wiped it away with the paper towel he had before him. He craned his neck, and looked past her to the wood-burning cast iron stove.

"Wow. I thought that's what it was, but wasn't sure. Haven't seen one of those in forever."

Cathy nodded as she wiped her hands on the towel next to the bowl. "Yeah. I try to minimize the number of appliances and such that run off electricity, so it doesn't tax my generator too much. It cooks pretty well."

Russell glanced to the light that dangled overhead, then to the lamps and other lights around the cabin which were sparse. "So, everything in here that is on is powered by a generator?"

Cathy confirmed with a bow of her head. "Yep. Good thing too since that CME hit the planet. Not sure of what all damage it did, but I imagine it probably brought down the grid."

Russell lifted his brow in curiosity. The tip of the spoon dunked below the juices of the soup and stayed there. "CME? Grid down? I'm not following."

Cathy wiped away the juices from her pink lips with the towel and swallowed the food. "Yeah. Coronal Mass Ejection. Meaning, in laymen terms, the earth was struck by a wave of gamma radiation that was ejected from the sun. It can overload the power grid. Fry transformers and such. Anything connected to long lines is toast. Fires can pop up all over the place. Hell on earth. I'm somewhat kidding about that last part. Anything plugged into an electrical outlet or that relies on electricity to operate is gone. It can even damage satellites and such. Which means no GPS, phones, or anything like that."

Powerless World

What Cathy said sounded farfetched. How could such an event do that to the power grid. He had no working knowledge of the effects of such an event, and had never even heard of a CME for that matter, so he was at a disadvantage. Still, she popped off the facts like she had in-depth dealings on the subject.

"How do you know all of this? Are you some kind of scientist or expert on space and weird anomalies?"

Cathy shook her head, then leaned back in her chair. "I am no expert or scientist. Not by any means. I've just studied the different ways our infrastructure could be taken out. Whether by EMP, electromagnetic pulse, or CME. One can't prepare for TEOTWAWKI without doing the research. When the shit hits the fan, it's better to be safe than sorry. Honestly, it's all fascinating and yet terrifying stuff if you think about it.

The news reported on the CME some before it struck earth a day or so ago. They weren't sure of the scope, and how much of an impact it was going to have on the planet. Can't be sure how much damage has been done, but since we, society in general, rely so heavy on electricity and technology, it probably isn't good. We were due for such an event to happen. Those that prepared for it will be far better off than those who hadn't."

"Prepared?" Russell countered.

Cathy clarified. "Me and my late husband were preppers. One of the reasons why we moved up here was to become self-sufficient. Being so reliant on electricity and such was soon to bite us, humanity, in the ass. That day might be here."

Russell didn't recall hearing about such things on the news, or anywhere else for that matter. Then again, when one wallows in self-loathing and drinks in their free time, there wasn't much room for anything else.

Still, what Cathy divulged was hard to digest. The fact that the planet could be hit by such an event boggled his mind. It didn't seem real, and yet, from recent events he had experienced, the plane going down and losing cell reception, it kind of made sense.

"You said this CME can interfere with satellites and such, right? Meaning, loss of cell reception and communications in general, correct?" Russell inquired.

Cathy nodded, then stood from the table. She grabbed her bowl and made for the sink. "That's correct. Cell phones, landline phones, and most other types of communications would go down. So, trying to reach someone right now probably isn't going to happen. I know. I've tried."

Russell leaned forward and dug the phone from the back pocket of his jeans. He stared at the disabled device with a long-defeated gaze and thought of Sarah. "If I needed to contact my wife in Boston, how could I do that?"

Cathy turned and leaned against the counter. "Like I said, using a cell phone or anything that relies on towers or satellites is a no go. They won't work. Not for a long while."

Russell dropped the phone on the table. He reeled from the defeating words that spilled from her lips without hesitation. "How long are we talking? Days? Weeks?"

Cathy shrugged, then stepped away from the sink. She bent down and retrieved Max's dish from the floor. Max sprung from the floor and walked beside Cathy as she dished out some stew in his bowl. He groaned and watched her every move with a vigilant gaze.

"Could be days, weeks, or even years. Don't know. Being a prepper, we always plan for the worst and hope for the best. I'm hoping for sooner rather than later for my daughter's sake. She never got into the whole prepper lifestyle, so she isn't as prepared. That's one of the reasons I'm going to load up and head to Philadelphia, to make sure she's all right."

Powerless World

Russell lost his appetite from the devesting news. He didn't know if she was right or not, but just the thought twisted his stomach into knots. Although, he knew he needed to eat to get his strength back.

The past day had beaten him down emotionally and physically, and it wasn't getting any better. Losing Tim and now being stranded away from Sarah with no way of being able to contact her didn't sit well with him.

Russell rubbed his hands up and down his face, then sighed. "And the hits just keep on coming. Worst trip ever."

Cathy set Max's bowl back on the floor, then looked to Russell's long face. "I was meaning to ask why you were out there. Most folks who go hiking and such are dressed properly and have gear with them. You didn't have either."

Russell's eye shined with sadness as he thought about Tim. He took a moment to gather himself before he spoke. "I was traveling with a friend in his plane. We experienced engine trouble, among other things. We crashed out there. He didn't make it. I barely got out before the plane slipped off the side of a cliff."

Cathy lowered her head in solace. "I'm sorry to hear that. You're lucky to be alive. I couldn't imagine what that must have been like."

Russell folded his arms across his chest. The reality of the situation set in and that old familiar itch stirred inside of him. It was a feeling he'd get when life became too much to bear, and he needed to take the edge off.

He wasn't equipped to deal with the heaviness of his friend's death, and what had apparently happened to the planet. A drink was what he craved, needed to weather the squall overtaking him.

"You wouldn't happen to have anything to drink, would you?"

Derek Shupert

CHAPTER THIRTEEN

SARAH

The darkness was never ending, an infinite ether that spanned in either direction. Aside from the light of her phone, and those of the passengers aboard the subway, the tunnel remained dark.

Silence grated on Sarah's nerves.

The unsettling feeling of being watched slithered over her body. The voices of Tom barking at her and the Creeper whispering horrible things filled her head. She knew they weren't there, but the sensation remained.

Sarah kept the Glock tucked in her waistband with her free hand resting on the grip. The last thing she wanted was to be ambling about in the dark and come across a cop who found her wielding a gun. Best to avoid any such surprises that could result in an accidental shooting of some kind.

Powerless World

The other passengers' lights from the subway had dimmed. Every step she took, it grew fainter. Sarah remembered Debbie mentioning a possible exit within the tunnel that led to a stairwell, but wasn't sure where or how far away it could be.

Movement close by grabbed Sarah's attention. It sounded like footsteps skulking about in the darkness, but she couldn't be sure. She flinched, then froze. She looked about with baited breath. Her heartbeat thumped inside her head as she searched for the source of the subtle sound. It was hard to pinpoint the location within the blackness.

She spun in a circle. The flashlight from her phone washed over the tunnel walls on either side, not finding a cause for the disturbance. The Glock stayed tucked in place, for now.

"Hello?" Sarah called out. Dread tainted her voice. Her hands trembled. "Who's there?"

She prayed a voice would answer back, then again, that thought sort of scared her since she couldn't lay eyes on whoever was stalking her. Considering the sort of troubles she had encountered recently, she was leery that it would be anything good.

More movement drew closer without a response which caused Sarah to breathe faster. She tried to stay calm, but that was easier said than done. Over the past couple of hours, things had descended into chaos without any explanation as to why, and it didn't look like it was going to get any better.

"Whoever is there, please respond. I am armed and will defend myself if need be," she warned.

Something brushed against Sarah's foot, then crawled over the top of her shoe. A yelp slipped from her lips as she jumped, then backed away. Her phone tilted to the ground and hunted for the cause of her panic.

A large rat scurried about, then stopped. It looked around for a few seconds before darting off toward the wall across from Sarah.

She grumbled under her breath. She hated rats, mice, and anything of the kind. Just thinking about the tiny rodents made her skin crawl, let alone having one make contact with her.

A shiver slid down Sarah's body. An unkempt feeling washed over her. The fact that large rodents were close at hand made her want to get out of the tunnel that much faster.

Sarah moved down the tracks at a good clip. She made sure to be cognizant of the rails incase the power came back on. The light from her phone shifted every which way as she took deep breaths.

Up ahead, she caught a brief glimpse of a door that was set up off the ground. Above the dull, gray, metal door was an EXIT sign.

Sarah crossed over the tracks and climbed up the raised concrete walkway. She stood in front of the door and looked it over. Off to the side was a call box that showed no signs of life. No lights or indicators that it had any power.

She pressed the lone steel bar in that ran the width of the entrance. The door resisted. Sarah pushed harder until it popped free. The hinges creaked loudly as she forced it open, the sound echoing through the hollowness of the space. It must had been some time since this exit had been used last.

Sarah lifted her phone in the air and swept the interior of the stairwell. She craned her neck, and skimmed over the concrete steps that led to what she hoped was the surface.

The heat hadn't dissipated, nor had the stagnant air within the suffocating environment.

Footfalls crunched over debris on the concrete from behind her as a low-toned voice spoke. "Did you find a way out?"

Powerless World

Sarah jumped, then turned around in a blink, her hand tugging on the Glock. She deflated against the jamb of the door as she caught sight of Chris. "Christ."

He stood next to the raised walkway while glancing up at her. He held up his hands in protest and took a step back. "Whoa. Sorry. Didn't mean to alarm you. I didn't feel comfortable with you walking alone down here. Not after what happened back in the car. You looked pretty shook up."

Sarah removed her hand from the grip of the Glock. A breath of tension spewed from her mouth as she nodded. "Thanks, but next time, don't sneak up on me."

"Duly noted," he responded. "So, does this lead to the surface?"

Sarah held the phone back up and peered inside the stairwell. The hint of light was visible within the veil of darkness that hung in the air.

"It must go all the way up to the street. I don't know where else it would go other than there." She peered back to the businessman, then nodded toward the subway. "Go let the others know we found a way out. I'll leave the door open and head up to see if I can find out what the hell has happened."

Chris bowed his head and stepped away. He stopped in place after taking a single step, then glanced back to Sarah. "I do appreciate what you did back there with that guy and getting us out. Guess we were lucky you had that gun."

Sarah nodded.

He made his way back to the subway where the cumulation of light had grown from the other passengers.

Lucky? That was the last thing Sarah felt. Remorse, anger, and a buttload of other words could better describe the situation back on the subway. Still, it was done, and she'd have to carry it around with her for the rest of her life.

Sarah scavenged a broken chunk of concrete from a cinderblock and wedged it between the jamb and the door. She didn't want it to close and couldn't wait for the other passengers. Her nerves were frazzled, and her hands wouldn't stop shaking. No matter how hard she fought to remain positive and focus on the task at hand, trepidation found its way inside her head. She had to get out of that stifling tunnel and to the expanse of the surface to relieve the angst that wouldn't leave her alone.

Loud thumps above echoed through the stairwell. Her gaze flitted to the darkness above, and she yelled out. "Down here."

The footfalls continued hammering what sounded like steel. Sarah shined the light at the flights of stairs and climbed. She raced up each flight. The palm of her hand guided her onward along the railing and kept her from tipping over the edge.

She was exhausted, and the lack of air circulating weighed heavily on her momentum. Deep, hard breaths fled from her mouth as she paused.

From below, Sarah could hear the voices of the other passengers from the tunnel. The lights from their phones shone into the stairwell.

Sarah got back on the move. The small thread of light she spotted from the ground floor of the stairwell grew larger the closer she got. She was relieved to be out of that underground prison, but also feared what she might find on the surface. Especially seeing as no help was in sight, and they hadn't been contacted by any authorities since the power had gone out.

Noises from the surface became clearer as Sarah hit the landing just below the set of large steel doors. She cocked her head to the side, and trained an attentive ear—horns blaring, people screaming, and other loud noises she couldn't make out. It was hard to decipher what was going on. Had the world ended while she was trapped underground?

Sarah gulped, then grabbed one of the rungs of the ladder before her. She turned the flashlight off on her phone, then secured it in the back pocket of her trousers. She adjusted her purse, that hung from her shoulder, and climbed upward.

Short work was made of the ladder as she reached the double steel doors. The voices from below clamored in excitement as they made their way up the concrete steps after her.

The palm of her hand slid over the surface of the door, searching for a handle or latch. Sarah pushed up on one side. The dense door split apart and lifted into the air. It was heavy but manageable.

Sarah continued pushing up until the door opened all the way. Sunlight beamed down into the darkness of the stairwell. Sarah diverted her gaze away from the surface, shielding her face from the blinding light. She had grown accustomed to the blackness of the tunnel and had to give her eyes a few moments to adjust.

The other portion of the steel door was tossed up and pushed to the side. It locked into place with a simple click. Sarah climbed the rest of the way out and stood on the sidewalk.

Chaos had gripped Boston. It didn't look like the same place Sarah last saw before entering the subway station.

The streets were filled with long, snaking lines of cars that sat idle. Traffic signals were null and void of any bright lights that controlled the flow of stagnate vehicles. Horns bellowed and people yelled from what few cars had passengers within the vehicles.

Smoke tainted the air, and caused Sarah's nose to crinkle. Explosions erupted in the distance, and she flinched. She skimmed over the buildings nearby with a lost, frantic look. Some of the structures were on fire and burned unchallenged.

The other passengers from the subway emerged from the ground to the spectacle. Chatters of disbelief and sniffles of terror fled the frightened group of survivors.

"Dear God. What has happened?" one passenger gasped.

"Have we been attacked?" another whimpered.

"It's finally happened. Those damn North Koreans have started World War 3," a loud, raspy voice yelled out. "The end is near."

The trepidation that swirled about was thick and made Sarah's stomach knot. She felt sick, lost, and alone in a world that had plummeted into madness within a blink.

A cop raced down the sidewalk toward the herd of passengers. Sarah stayed planted and waved her arms at the stone-faced man. His hand rested on the grip of the Glock 22 he had secured in its holster.

"Excuse me, officer," Sarah called out while flagging him down. "Can you tell me-"

The cop skirted around Sarah without missing a beat. He didn't glance her way or acknowledge her presence. She turned on her heels and watched him shove his way through the other people who traveled along the sidewalk. He vanished around the corner of the next street.

Sarah rubbed her hands up and down her face, lost in a sea of confusion and uncertainty. The world had gone to hell in a handbag, and she was now forced to sift through the aftermath.

Powerless World

CHAPTER FOURTEEN

RUSSELL

A powerless world. What did that even mean?

Russell fought with the possible outcome Cathy had laid out before him. It didn't seem real, or even feasible, but yet, something had happened.

Cathy washed the few dishes she had in the sink, then turned toward him. She didn't have any alcohol in the cabin. Even if she had, it wouldn't have helped Russell since he had various medicines swimming in his system. Drinking while on painkillers was never a good recipe, and she advised him as much.

She pointed at the stew before Russell. "You should finish that. You need to build your strength up."

Russell couldn't. His appetite had passed. He sat there, slouched in the chair, with his palms flat on his thighs. He dug his hand into the front pocket of his jeans and pulled out a stick of gum. He removed the wrapper and shoved the gum into his mouth.

"I appreciate the food, but I've lost my appetite."

Cathy reached across the table and took the bowl. "You're welcome. If you want more here in a bit, I can get you a bowl. I'm going to throw it out before I get on the road tomorrow morning, so I'd like to minimize the waste."

Russell peered out of the window to the dense woods beyond the cabin. He focused on the green foliage that surrounded the trunks of the large trees. He needed to clear his head and figure out what his next move was going to be.

"I think I'm going to get some fresh air." Russell scooted his chair back, then stood up. He grabbed his phone from the table, then turned toward the entrance to the cabin.

Max trotted over to his side. He stopped shy of the screen door and stared through the wire mesh. He fidgeted in place. Max tilted his head back and looked to Russell with a serious expression.

"What's up with the dog?" Russell asked while pointing at the rigid stance of the large German Shepherd.

Cathy craned her neck and looked over at Max. "He probably caught wind of an animal. It happens all the time. He's got a nose like you wouldn't believe. Would you mind letting him out? He probably needs to use the restroom, anyway. He likes to go after eating."

"Yeah. No problem." Russell opened the screen door. Max bolted from the cabin and leapt from the porch. His bushy tail wagged to and fro as he sniffed the ground.

The brisk, clean air of the mountains brushed over Russell's face as he walked outside. It didn't smell dirty like the city, which was swollen with exhaust and other bad smells Russell had grown accustomed to. Instead, it smelt of pine and had a rich earthy scent that filled the air. It was refreshing, and something Russell soaked in.

The rickety boards of the porch squeaked under him as he crossed them to the grass in front of the log house.

Max milled about the trees, sniffing and investigating the thickets and dense brush. His ears stood on end as he searched for the perfect place to relieve himself.

Russell thumbed the power button to his phone, hoping that the device would fire up. The screen sat blank for a few seconds before the manufacture logo splashed on the screen. It was distorted and not as clear as it should be, but it was working at least.

Max barked, then emerged from the dense verdure. He darted out of the bushes and galloped across the yard as if in pursuit of something. Russell couldn't spot what had sparked his interest, but chalked it up to a squirrel, rabbit, or some other wild animal.

The phone dinged and finished loading. The device scanned for a signal, but couldn't locate one. Russell opened the gallery of pictures stored on the memory card of his phone.

A picture of Jess and Sarah filled the screen—the two women in his life who meant the world to him. He thumbed through the remainder of the photos, reliving the good times that were now distant memories.

Max barked again, then growled. It was faint, but loud enough for him to be close by. Something had his full attention and wasn't letting him go.

Russell pocketed the phone and walked around the front of the cabin. A long row of chopped wood spanned the side of the house. It sat waist high and had a blue tarp that draped over the top.

A winding dirt drive climbed up the steep embankment, and vanished beyond the trees that encompassed the property. Russell looked about and didn't spot a vehicle of any kind. On the other side of the drive was a large, barn-like structure that had ruts in the ground. They vanished under the two large wooden doors.

Max barreled around the building, barking and pawing at the wooden slats. He paused, low to the ground, and dug at the base with his front paws.

Russell skimmed over the dense woods. The heavy vegetation and tall weeds made it difficult to see.

Max looked toward Russell with a stern look. His ears stood erect as he lifted his front paw off the ground.

"What is it?" Russell called out as he walked across the driveway.

Max moved around to the front of the barn. He stood on his hind legs and pressed against the doors with his front paws.

Russell petted Max's head as he lowered to the ground. He groaned and kept his focus glued to the building. Russell looked over the barn, then took a step back. He peered toward the roof as a loud clanging noise echoed from inside the structure.

He grabbed the rusted handles of the barn doors and pulled. They bulged some before snapping to. "Hello? Is someone in there?"

Russell listened for a response, but didn't receive one. He glanced to the side and made for the corner of the wooden structure.

Is there someone else living here that Cathy failed to mention? Russell pondered.

Max turned toward the driveway, and barked at the ridge where the dirt road vanished beyond the tree line. He took off in a dead sprint, barking at whatever lurked beyond the foliage.

Russell skirted the corner of the building and peered down the side. A handful of saw horses and a wheelbarrow were overtaken by the grass that grew around them.

A path of paver stones sat in the ground at Russell's feet. They ran the length of the building and stopped toward the rear. He followed the walkway, listening for any additional sounds.

He peered over his shoulder at the cabin, scanning for Cathy or Max. Neither were in sight. He reached the end of the barn and discovered a door.

The glass was thick with grime that had built up over the four sections of small windows. Russell leaned forward with the ridge of his hand above his brow. He squinted, trying to see inside the dark, ominous structure.

He couldn't spot what made the noise from the gunk caked on the windows. Russell rubbed his elbow over the glass, trying to clean off a portion to allow him to see inside the building. He tilted his head to the side, dipped his chin, then grabbed the doorknob.

Russell twisted it clockwise. A branch snapped and pulled him away from the window. He stood up straight, looking for Max or Cathy.

The door flew outward without warning and smashed into Russell's face. The blow knocked him off balance, and he stumbled backward. His hand left the doorknob as a large, shadowy figure stomped out of the building.

"What the-"

The man punched Russell in the face. He hit the ground with a dense thud. His eyes watered from the blow, distorting his vision.

Footfalls through the grass filled Russell's ears. The assailant's fingers grabbed handfuls of his flannel shirt and jerked him off the ground.

Russell swung at the brute. He blinked, trying to erase the tears that hindered his vision.

The report of a gunshot fired off close to the dueling men. Max barked and raced down the driveway as Cathy ran toward the barn with her rifle shouldered.

The man paused, then glanced toward Cathy. He released his hold from Russell's shirt and fled into the woods.

Max rounded the corner of the barn and stopped just shy of Russell. He licked his face. The crunching of leaves and snapping of branches perked his ears.

"Max, stay," Cathy commanded as he skirted around Russell. She came to a grinding halt as Russell laid prone on his back. "Are you ok?"

Russell groaned as trickles of blood ran from his nose. He looked to the wooden area where the attacker had fled. "Yeah. I'm good. Wasn't expecting that, though."

Cathy took a knee with Max by her side. She swept the tree line with her rifle. Her face twisted in anger, and her brow furrowed.

Her full, pink lips grew taut as she huffed. "Damn trespassers."

Max groaned and whined. He inched forward with his gaze fixed in the direction the man fled.

Cathy snapped her fingers. "Max, stay."

Russell picked himself off the ground. Dirt and grass clung to his clothes. He brushed away the earth as Cathy stood up. "Do you know who that was?"

Cathy lowered her rifle. The buttstock rested against her hip with the barrel trained at the semi-cloudy sky. She sighed, then rubbed her hand over her face in frustration. "Yeah. I have a good idea of who it was. One of Marcus Wright's backwoods friends."

Max remained by her side, poised to strike and defend. His ears twitched with any subtle noise that loomed from the dense woods. His head shifted from side to side.

Russell turned and pointed at the open door of the barn. "Is that where you keep your car? Whoever attacked me was in their doing something. Not sure if they were messing with it or not, though."

Cathy sighed again, then growled under her breath as she slung the rifle over her shoulder. She stomped past Russell and stormed inside the building. "Bastards. They have been hounding me for my property for as long as I can remember. Not so much for the house, but more for the land. They've tried bribing me to sign over my deed. When that didn't work, they resorted to more dubious tactics like what you just saw. Coming on my property and messing with stuff. Scare tactics to make me leave. It's ramped up since my husband passed. I've put in complaints with the sheriff's office, but that doesn't seem to have stopped it. Not that the sheriff would take it serious or anything since they're all buddies."

Russell followed Cathy into the building and stood inside the doorway. It was damp and dark. A lone window on the far wall was the only source of light.

In the middle of the structure was an older model Jeep. The dark-green car had mud caked to its sides. Clumps of dirt and grass hung from the undercarriage. Four large off-road tires had the beast jacked up off the ground.

"Why would they want just the land, and not the house and everything else?"

Cathy milled about the space. She skimmed over the shelves of tools and other items. Max pushed his way past Russell. He sniffed the ground around the tires of the Jeep, then moved to the far side.

"Marcus is pissed that we got this land. Said we snatched it out from under him. He complained and moaned that his family had ownership rights to it, but he could never prove it. We went to court and he lost. Needless to say, he's a sore loser and hasn't moved on." Cathy skirted the front of the Jeep and stopped. "Would you mind popping the hood?"

"Yeah. Sure." Russell walked to the driver's side of the vehicle and opened the door. He reached under the dash and popped the hood. "If they're causing so many problems for you, why not sell it to them and be done with it. Doesn't seem worth the headache."

Cathy lifted the cover as Russell moved to the front of the Jeep. "Because. I don't take kindly to being threatened and pushed around by anyone. I'm not some dainty, helpless female, and I will not be bullied out of my home."

She stood on the tips of her toes and scanned over the engine. There wasn't much light, which made it difficult to make anything out.

"I've got my phone with me. It's got a decent flashlight on it."

Cathy dismissed the offer with a wave of her hand. "Thanks, but I got it covered."

She retrieved a small flashlight from the shelf of a metal rack near her. She thumbed the switch and waved the blinding light over the engine compartment.

Max brushed against her leg, then mine. He panted as he rested on his haunches while facing the opened door to the building—a sentry on watch.

"Do you think they messed with the Jeep?" Russell inquired.

Cathy shrugged. Her hand traced over the cables as she skimmed over the greasy parts. "Don't know. Wouldn't put it past them, though. The more time that goes by, the bolder they seem to get. I'm leaving tomorrow and need this tin can operational."

Russell looked away and scanned over the aged workbench against the wall next to him. The top was covered with various engine parts and liquids. Brake fluid, oil, and windshield wiper fluid rounded out the assortment.

"So, you do all of the upkeep and maintenance on the Jeep?"

Cathy nodded, then stepped back from the engine. "Yeah. The nearest garage is in Luray, which isn't too close. Besides, I've learned to rely on myself. Can't live in such a remote place without being able to take care of such things. Watch your hands."

Russell moved away as Cathy slammed the hood down. She wiped the grime and dirt from her palms on her jeans.

"Is it good to go?" Russell asked as she walked by him.

Cathy jerked open the driver's side door, then scaled the side of the beast. She leaned back in the seat and pulled out a set of keys. "Guess we'll find out."

She slipped the key into the ignition, then pumped the gas. The engine grumbled at first, but then smoothed out. The smell of exhaust filled the building in a blink, causing Russell to cough on the fumes.

The Jeep idled free of any issues which made Cathy breathe a sigh of relief. She revved the engine which responded without hesitation.

Cathy peered down to Max and Russell, then gave a thumbs up. She killed the engine and removed the key. She hopped down from the Jeep, and slammed the door shut.

"Looks like we're good. It doesn't appear that they did anything to the engine. They may have stopped when they heard you and Max."

That was good news, and just what Russell wanted to hear. She had a working vehicle, and he needed a way to get back to Boston. Since they were heading in the same direction, Russell figured they could team up and help each other out.

He cleared his throat as Cathy shoved the keys back into the pocket of her jeans. She brushed the strands of loose hair away from her sweaty face, then placed her hands on her hips.

"Since you're heading north, would you mind if I tagged along with you and Max?"

Powerless World

Cathy stared at Russell for a moment. She peered down to Max who was by his side. He looked up at her, waiting for orders. "Yeah. I can take you as far as Philly. After that, you'll have to find another way to Boston."

Russell nodded. "Sounds good."

Derek Shupert

CHAPTER FIFTEEN

SARAH

The passengers had all but scattered, setting off into a city that had been ravaged by some sort of major event. There was no law and order, just random acts of violence and destruction that swallowed the crumbling society.

Sarah couldn't believe the tumult before her. Buildings were ransacked. TVs and other valuables were hauled off through the busted windows by looters. Hordes of people scurried away like rodents with their spoils.

The few cops who could be seen struggled to wrangle the deviants who took advantage of the chaos. They were outnumbered and overwhelmed by the mass influx of vandals who sought to exploit the strained police force.

Sarah pulled her shirt down over the Glock she had secured in her waistband, fearing that some unsavory thug might try to snatch it. Her gaze shifted to the frantic people who darted past her. Their faces were thick with terror and uncertainty. She grabbed the strap of her purse a hair tighter and wormed her way through the crowd.

Copley Place was her destination, although, she wasn't sure if her friend, Mandy, would still be there considering what had transpired. She hated being cut off from her friends and family while the world around her fell apart.

The intersection up ahead swarmed with parked cars. Horns blared as people screamed and yelled at one another from the interiors of the vehicles. They jockeyed for position, trying to worm their way through the chaos. Most of the vehicles sat abandoned, creating a larger problem for those who remained with their rides.

"Excuse me, ma'am," a woman yelled, and waved from the corner of the building Sarah was approaching. "Do you know what's going on here?"

Sarah approached with caution. The oversized purse she carried was pressed to her chest as her gaze lurked on the sea of parked cars and scrambling people.

"I have no clue. Me and a bunch of other folks were trapped in the subway tunnel when it lost power. We got out a bit ago on our own. Help never arrived." A group of people rushed past Sarah and the woman. They bumped into the two women and continued on their way at a brisk pace. "Were we bombed or something? The ground shook. It felt like an explosion went off."

The woman shrugged as she leaned into the brick wall of the building they were huddled against. "I don't know about any bombs, but there were two airliners that crashed. One went down a few blocks to the east. The other further south. Craziest thing I'd ever seen. They collided in mid-air and the wreckage rained down over the city. There was a big fireball from the point of impact.

Not sure if the fire department was able to make it over there with all of the traffic and other fires going."

Sarah's face scrunched in shock. Tiny explosions could be heard in the distance. She turned on her heels and looked to the east. Black smoke lifted over the sprawling buildings and filled the air. The explosions could've been what she smelled when first exiting the emergency stairwell from the subway tunnel.

"How in the world would two large airliners just crash into one another?" Sarah posed. "Don't they have radar or something similar to let them know where other aircrafts are in the sky?"

"No clue," the woman retorted. "I just know what I saw and heard. It feels almost biblical."

Gunfire rang out down the street. Multiple shots echoed throughout the canyon of buildings. The woman flinched, then yelped. She lowered her head and cradled her belongings.

Sarah craned her neck, searching for the source of the gunfire. It was hard to pinpoint with all of the chaos around them.

People screamed, and raced down the bustling street in droves, but she couldn't spot what had them spooked and running scared.

"We need to get out of here," Sarah said. "It's a damn war-"

A tall man dressed in ratty jeans and a tattered, black hoodie that concealed most of his face, grabbed the woman's bag.

"Hey," she cried out in protest.

The man jerked the straps of the purse, fighting to rip it free of her grasp. He grunted and growled while shooting Sarah an angered expression from the depths of the cloth covering his head.

His face was sullen with a black, wiry beard. An ungodly stench radiated from the rags draped over his rail-thin frame.

"Let her stuff go, you piece of shit," Sarah barked as she reached for his arm.

The man pulled the bag away from the woman and pushed her back to the wall. He turned toward Sarah and snarled. He smacked her with the back of his hand, knocking her flat on her ass.

Pain lanced through Sarah's jaw, then spread through the rest of her face. She hadn't been struck in such a manner before. Shock turned to anger. Her brow furrowed as she rubbed her cheek. That feeling of being helpless and threatened by an opposing force made her blood boil.

The attacker grabbed Sarah's purse and slipped it off her shoulder. She reached for the straps, and fought to keep it from him, but it was ripped from her grasp. He back-peddled down the sidewalk, then turned about and ran away. The woman raced after him, screaming at the thug who had just robbed her and Sarah of their valuables.

"Help. Anybody, help."

Those who were within earshot turned a blind eye and kept to themselves.

Sarah pulled herself off the sidewalk and ran after both. Her head throbbed with every step she took, but she pushed on. Tears distorted her vision enough to hinder her being able to keep a close eye on the thug.

She brushed the back of her hand across her eyes, trying to wipe away the wetness that coated them.

He ran at a good clip, shoving his way through the people that stood in his way.

The woman stayed a few paces back. Her hands waved in the air as she screamed obscenities at the thief. No police were in sight. If they had been, would they have helped?

Powerless World

Sarah figured given the state of unrest and the decline of civility among the populous, the odds of obtaining any help from the authorities was going to be a long shot.

The thief cut to the right and vanished down the alley next to Frank's Sandwich Shop. The woman's golden-brown hair bounced from side to side as she trampled the concrete. She rounded the corner at full speed as Sarah fought to close the gap. The further away the thief got, the less likely she'd be able to get her ID and other belongings back.

An older man raised his hand in the air next to the sandwich shop. "Ma'am, do you know—"

Sarah brushed past him without breaking her stride. She hugged the corner of the brick building and darted down the alleyway in a dead heat. She stomped through puddles of water and skirted around dumped over trash cans. Sarah didn't see the thug, or the distraught woman for that matter, but she could hear the woman's pleas for help.

A loud screech echoed down the alleyway. The woman stumbled out from behind a dark-green dumpster while cradling her stomach. Blood soaked the front of her tan sweater. Her face twisted in a look of shock as she dropped to her knees.

The vile degenerate emerged from the side of the large steel container with their bags in one hand and a knife in the other.

Tears streamed down the woman's cheeks. The black mascara she wore left dark patches under both eyes with long, snaking lines that slithered down to her chin.

Sarah reached for her Glock and pulled it free of her waistband. Anger swelled inside her stomach at the sickening scene. She couldn't believe what the low-life had done.

The man in the black hoody scurried away. Sarah's arm bounced all over as she struggled to get the fleeing thug in her sights. She had never fired the Glock while on the run, and didn't want to waste the ammo or run the risk of hitting the injured woman by accident.

The woman dumped over onto her side while clutching her stomach. Her large eyes shined with fright as Sarah stopped and assessed the wound. Tears ran down the sides of the scared woman's face. Her shaking hands palmed the gash in her gut, trying to stay the flow of blood that pumped from her body.

"Holy Christ," Sarah muttered while staring at the thick, sanguine fluid. She was unsure of what to do. The woman shook as if chilled to the marrow. "Help. Can anybody help."

Sarah glanced to the street, but found no help. Any people who darted past the passageway didn't offer a curious gaze their way.

The woman removed one of her hands and grabbed Sarah's arm. Blood smeared over the fabric of her clothes. She mumbled incoherent nonsense through quivering lips.

Flashbacks of the night Jess had been stabbed by the home intruder filled her gaze. The helplessness of losing her baby girl stoked the fires of regret and rage within her core as she peered at the dying woman.

The discord of steel trash cans crashing and rolling across the alley echoed through the tight corridor. Sarah's gaze flitted away from the woman, and spotted the man in the black hoody picking up the contents from the bags he had dropped. He was manic and kept peering over his shoulder in her direction.

The woman's breathing was shallow.

The filthy water under her body became dark and rich with blood.

Sarah laid the woman down, then looked to the man who scooped up the remaining items from the ground. She had grown tired of being a victim and was going to handle the low-life herself, one way or another.

CHAPTER SIXTEEN

RUSSELL

The light was dying.

The remainder of the day in the Blue Ridge Mountains had been uneventful. Cathy spent her time packing up her belongings while Max stood watch at the screen door like a sentry. He laid on his stomach with his gaze scanning the nearby woods for any movement. His ears twitched as short growls loomed from his snout.

Russell sat at the table with a cup of coffee cradled in his hands. Steam from the rich, black brew filled his nose. He took a sip, then glanced out of the window in the kitchen.

The sun dipped behind the wooden mountain ranges. Its orange, fiery glow diminished with each second that went by.

Cathy lit candles she had positioned around the log house. The glow from the flames brought life to the darkening space. What natural light remained was soon consumed by the murk.

Powerless World

Russell turned in his seat, then rested his forearm on top of the wooden chair's back. "You sure I can't help you with anything?"

Cathy stooped in front of the reddish-brown brick fireplace. She piled stacks of chopped wood on the sheets of newspaper that blanketed the steel hearth. "I've got most everything ready. We just need to load the Jeep up in the morning. I figure we'll cut out of here around first light."

Max glanced toward Cathy and lowered his ears. His tongue rolled out of his snout as if he were smiling at her.

Russell took another sip from the coffee as Cathy ignited a long match. The head sparked and fire lifted from the rounded end. She placed the dancing flame around the ends of the paper.

The fire consumed the paper in a matter of seconds. It spread to the logs underneath as Cathy retrieved the steel poker. She shifted the logs around, which made the fire blossom.

Everything Cathy did seemed as though it was second nature. There was no hesitation or uncertainty with any task that faced her. Not only was she tough, but from what Russell could tell, she had a good head on her shoulders.

"How long have you been doing this prepper thing?" Russell asked.

Cathy continued to shift and maneuver the logs until the fire burned to her liking. She stood and secured the poker in the stand to the side of the fireplace.

"I've been a prepper for some time. Can't remember how long, though. It's more of a lifestyle than anything. I've always liked living off the land and being around nature. The concrete jungle never appealed to me. The stench of exhaust and the noise of cars got on my nerves. Once Amber turned eighteen, my late husband, Bill, and I built this house, and sold the one we had in the city." Cathy took a seat in one of the chairs near the fireplace.

117

Max stood up, gave his thick coat a good shake, then trotted away from the screen door. He moved across the living room and plopped down by Cathy's feet near the fireplace.

The slight breeze blowing into the cabin sent a shiver through Russell. He took another hearty sip of coffee and made his way to the couch.

The warmth of the fire spread throughout the cabin, erasing the bite of the cool night air. The orange glow of the flames danced in his eyes as he took a seat on the firm couch.

"I can't say that I've ever been around anyone who lived this far away from civilization and liked it. Most of the people I know have a different idea to "roughing" it. Not sure how they'd fair with no electricity and being reliant on their own survival skills as a way of life."

Cathy nodded in agreement. "I have friends that are that way. They couldn't believe we were going to live in such a remote place. Neither could Amber. She's a city girl. Always has been. She's smart and has good instincts, so generally I don't worry about her. With all of this happening, though, and not being able to contact her, it just has me on edge. I know how folks can get during times of crisis. Even good people can do bad things when they're scared and unsure of what's going on."

The riots and natural disasters that happened from years past were a prime example of that. Once the SHTF, people would lose their minds and chaos would ensue.

Max groaned, then yawned. He stretched out his legs and rolled onto his side. His tongue licked around his snout as he breathed a heavy sigh through his nose.

Russell pointed at Max. "You did a good job training him. He listens and obeys well."

Cathy leaned forward and glanced down to the resting German shepherd. "He used to be a military dog. I got him after Bill passed away. It was more for the company, but it didn't hurt that he had already been trained as he was. He fits me pretty well."

Russell agreed. German shepherds were great dogs. Loyal and protective to the end. "Well, it seems like a good fit. He's a good pup."

Max groaned some more as Cathy bent over. She ran her nails along the side of his coat. His tail wagged as he sat there and relished in the attention he was receiving. "Do you and your wife have any kids or pets?"

Kids? That was a loaded question. One that Russell figured was coming considering the nature of their conversation. He took another sip from the mug he had clutched between both of his hands as the flames from the fireplace danced in his eyes.

"Pets, no. At least, not for many years, now. We had a daughter. Jess. She passed away about a year ago, though."

Sadness washed over Cathy's face as she dipped her chin. She sat back in her chair and looked at Russell who stared off into space. "Oh my. I'm so sorry to hear that. I can't imagine how hard that must've been for the both of you. When I lost Bill to cancer, it devastated me and took me some time to finally accept what had happened and be able to move on."

Russell downed the remainder of coffee that sloshed about in the bottom of his mug. He offered Cathy a tilt of his head and a warm smile. After all, he didn't want to be rude seeing what all she had done for him.

"Thanks. I appreciate it. It's been difficult for me to move on, even after a year, but I'm managing the best I can. My wife, Sarah, has done a better job of processing everything. She just wishes that I'd open up and let her in. I can get pretty guarded and defensive about it."

Russell didn't hide the pain that he battled too well, which he knew. His body shifted his weight as he'd become antsy. He'd tap his foot and divert his gaze as to not make eye contact. It was getting better, and something that he would address once he got back to Boston.

"That is understandable. We all process grief in different ways. There is no set path that we take, and certainly, no time limit to healing. But having your wife by your side will be more helpful than going at it alone."

It was true and something that Russell already knew, but the guilt that clung to his soul fought to keep him down. He had an uphill battle ahead of him and was ready to tackle it head on.

CHAPTER SEVENTEEN

SARAH

The man in the black hoody had made a huge mistake. He just didn't know it yet.

Sarah trailed the gutless low-life as best she could through the maze of alleys that snaked through the aged buildings. They both ran at a good clip, neither yielding to the other.

The Glock remained fixed within Sarah's grasp. She narrowed her gaze at the clumsy hoodlum who struggled to keep his legs under him. He wasn't going to get away.

It was hard to tell if he was uncoordinated or on drugs. From his gaunt frame and the brief glimpse she got at his sallow face, it made her think he might be a meth head. That could be why he stole their belongings. He needed a fix in the worst way and was low on cash. After all, most people seemed to think women were easy targets.

121

Rays of sunshine dwindled to a darkening haze that hovered overhead. Smoke tainted the air wherever they went. Sarah could taste the bitterness of it.

Sarah was growing tired of running, but letting him get away with murder and her property wasn't an option. All she could see was Jess lying in their living room, bleeding out from the gash the intruder dealt across her mid-section. Nothing made Sarah feel more helpless than watching her only child pass in her arms.

Hoody darted out of the alleyway while glancing over his shoulder. He wasn't paying attention. Beams of light traced along the Clarendon Street Garage walls. The sound of water splashed as a four-door sedan came into view.

The vehicle slammed its brake. Hoody jumped onto the hood of the car with a dense thud. The purse of the woman he'd killed slid across the car and vanished on the other side.

The driver of the sedan threw open his door. A plump, bald-headed man stepped out. He stood behind the door, yelling and pumping his fist at the air. "What the hell. Are you ok, pal? I could've run you over."

Hoody limped around the front of the sedan toward the parking garage without looking in the irate man's direction. The man continued yelling from the driver's side before catching wind of footfalls hammering his way. He looked back toward the alleyway in search of what was charging his way.

Sarah skirted the front of the sedan at a steady clip.

Hoody hobbled inside the parking garage as Sarah closed in. She raced up the steep incline of the entrance to the first floor of the structure.

The thug's footfalls echoed throughout the covered parking lot, then faded to nothing. She had lost sight of him within the dimness. Any sunlight that was left struggled to touch the interior of the space.

Sarah paused, then listened. Her heart thumped inside her head as she gasped for air. Both legs ached. Her muscles burned. Skipping the gym for the past year had caught up to her.

She skimmed over the cars that were parked in the structure. If she couldn't locate him quickly, she'd have to cut her losses and leave if she was going to get to Mandy's place. That notion made her mad, and caused her to grind her teeth.

Where are you, you bastard?

Sarah turned on her heels, sweeping the dark interior from side to side. A choice had to be made on which way to go.

A subtle noise from her left caught Sarah's ear. She turned, and looked for the hoody, but found nothing.

The squealing of tires from the upper levels sounded off. Slow and steady, and with the Glock up and at the ready, Sarah advanced.

Her moist palms repositioned over the grip. Beads of sweat raced down from her hairline. The inside of her mouth was dry, and felt as though it was stuffed with cotton. She needed water, but it would have to wait.

Sarah skimmed over the parked cars on both sides of her, sweeping the spaces between them. Any fear that tried to take hold was held at bay by sheer will.

A slight tremor in her hands caused the Glock to shake. Adrenaline spiked through her veins. Contempt for the scum's violent act of killing that woman propelled her on. She took in another deep breath, trying to focus her nerves.

A car engine revved, followed by squealing tires from behind her. Sarah turned just as the headlights from a truck barreled around the corner at the other end of the garage. The driver pushed the vehicle with reckless abandon and sped toward the entrance of the parking structure. It dipped down the ramp and vanished to the street below.

The silhouette of a figure rushed out from behind one of the vehicles near Sarah. The footfalls of the approaching threat flanking her sent a bolt of adrenaline through her body.

Heavy, labored breaths escaped the man's lips as he closed the gap. Sarah turned to the side as hoody grabbed her from behind, restricting her movement.

His meager arms wrapped around her chest, pulling her body closer to him. A foul stench blew from his mouth with every grunt.

He reached for the Glock. Sarah stomped his foot with the heel of her shoe. A squelch of pain left his lips as his hold loosened.

Sarah wiggled her body free and stepped forward. She elbowed her attacker in the gut, then spun around. A swift strike to his genitals sent the hoodlum crumbling to the pavement.

"Damn, lady. My nuts." His voice cracked and raised an octave. He curled into the fetal position and whined.

"Serves you right, you piece of crap." Sarah kicked him in the gut twice, feeling justified for her actions. "Where the hell is my purse?" Sarah knelt next to the man, searching for her belongings. She grabbed his arm and pulled him over to his back. Her purse sat on the ground. She reached across and snatched the loops. It felt like everything was there, but she wasn't sure and would have to wait before sifting through the contents.

Her finger caressed the trigger of the Glock. The barrel trained at the man's head. His face was cloaked within the hood, but the whimpers that loomed from within conveyed he was afraid of dying.

"Please, don't kill me," he beseeched.

"Did that woman you stab ask that of you?" she barked with a hoarse growl. "YOU attacked us. YOU killed that women when

124

all she wanted was HER property back. It's vile scum like you that makes me sick to my stomach."

The Glock trembled in Sarah's hand. A sheen of wetness coated her eyes. She wasn't a cold-blooded killer. Far from it, but she had done what was needed to protect herself from the scourge of society. From the Creeper to the homely man on the subway, and now to the hooded degenerate who had robbed a woman of her life and Sarah's own security, she had been pushed to her breaking point.

Hoody remained flat on his back with his hands in the air. A scared, sad excuse for a human being who now knew what it felt like to be powerless, and at the mercy of another.

Despite that feeling of rage and loss, Sarah couldn't pull the trigger. She regretted having shot the homely man. It shouldn't have happened, much like this scenario and Jess's death. All of it was senseless, which made it that much worse.

Sarah lowered the Glock, then took a hearty step back. The firearm hung by her side as her finger rested against the trigger. Contempt, fear, and sadness all washed over her in that moment. Although she had decided she couldn't kill an unarmed man who was no longer a threat, Sarah was ready to do what was needed if he tried anything.

Hoody didn't move. He stayed prone on his back. The whimpers faded away as he sat up from the ground. The palms of both his hands pressed the pavement as he glanced up to her.

"Thank you for not shooting me," he sputtered.

"Shut up," Sarah snapped. Her voice was cold and callous. She kicked him in the stomach once more to vent the pent-up stress that swelled deep in her gut. It felt good having reclaimed her power back from the cowering man. "Don't thank me just yet. You're going to pay for what you did."

"What are you going to do—to me?" His voice cracked. It was shaken and unsteady.

Sarah reached around to her back pant pocket and snagged her phone. She thumbed the power button, then turned the flashlight on. "Remove your hood, now."

The light from the phone washed over his faded, dingy hoody and soiled jeans.

Hoody sat there, still and motionless.

Sarah trained the Glock at his skull. He flinched. She shifted the Glock an inch or two to the side and pointed it at the pavement.

Five pounds of pressure. That's all it took. Sarah remembered hearing that in her firearms class. That's all that was required to end a person's life, or save it. It was a simple phrase that repeated every time she thought of pulling the trigger.

A single round popped off and struck the pavement near his hand. Hoody screeched. His hands flew up in front of him as the white flash from the muzzle framed the angular man's trembling body.

The sharp report echoed through the parking garage, then faded away.

"I'm not going to ask again. Remove the damn hood," Sarah growled.

The vandal snapped to, grabbed a handful of the dense fabric, and yanked the hood back. His wild black hair went every which way. Both eyes were sunken into his skull. The wiry strands of coarse hair poked out from his unkept beard in a disorganized manner.

Sarah lined up the criminal in her sights and switched on the camera. The light vanished. She took three pictures, one right after the other. The camera flashed, then clicked, recording the snapshots. He didn't budge.

Powerless World

The images displayed on her screen which was growing dim. Battery life was diminishing, but Sarah felt it was worth it. All three photos looked good. She'd share it with the authorities once she had the chance.

Sarah moved past him and headed in the direction of the exit that led to the street below. She watched his every move as she pocketed the phone in her trousers. The barrel of the Glock lined up with his skull, discouraging any sort of haphazard thought that might gel in his head.

He stayed planted on his backside, watching with a resigned gaze. She could no longer see his face, only the odd shape of his head and the thick, matted strands of hair that stuck out.

Sarah drifted farther away, then raced down the ramp to the empty street below. She hooked the corner of the concrete wall that ran in front of the parking garage in a dead sprint.

She was relieved to have gotten her property back and a picture of the hoodlum who belonged in jail. Sarah was glad she didn't kill him, even though he had murdered someone in cold blood. She was no longer going to be an easy target.

For those who would look to prey on her, they would soon find out as much.

Derek Shupert

CHAPTER EIGHTEEN

RUSSELL

Weathering the storm was easier said than done. It took willpower and grit, something Russell wasn't sure he had much of.

The gum had lost its flavor. His jaw hurt from chewing. It helped at first, but the sticks of soggy gum couldn't replace the need for a stiff, cold drink. Especially right now.

The cabin had grown silent. Cathy and Max had retreated to her bedroom about an hour or so ago. Early to bed, early to rise and all that jazz. Cathy didn't say it, but she didn't need to. She had plans for getting the day started at first light which Russell was all for.

Hell, they could've left sooner, and he would've been happy with that. Not knowing how his wife was doing, or if she was safe, kept him on edge.

Derek Shupert

Russell paced about the cabin with his arms folded across his chest. Certain planks in the floor creaked and gave under his weight which was annoying. It didn't bother Cathy or Max, but still, the sharp sound grated on his nerves.

The fire in the hearth dwindled down to a small, pitiful flame, which reduced the amount of light in the cabin. The logs Cathy used from before was all that had been added. They were nothing more now than charred pieces of wood. Russell didn't bother adding more. There was no need. The front door had been shut, cutting off the bite of the wind that blew through the screen door. The house was warm and comfortable.

Russell rubbed his hands over his haggard face as he walked to the kitchen. There had to be a bottle of feel good somewhere in the cabinets. He had no plans of getting wasted. A taste was all he needed to set his mind, and body, at ease.

He checked each cabinet, opening the doors with a gentle touch. He glanced over his shoulder at Cathy's room for any reaction to the squeaking hinges. No response was given.

All were barren of what Russell craved. He sighed, then grumbled under his breath. His hands quaked from the lack of alcohol swimming through his veins. It wasn't bad, yet. A single taste would cure what ailed him.

A twinge of pain from his injuries flared. Rotating his shoulder hurt some, but it was getting better. The bite from the mountain lion throbbed some, but was bearable.

It had been some time since he had taken any painkillers. That was by design. He hoped that he'd happen across a bottle of liquor and didn't want to have any more medication in his system. He knew Cathy was right about mixing such things. Doing so would only compound any problems he faced.

Damn it.

130

Powerless World

The palms of Russell's hands rested against the edge of the counter. His head dangled in defeat. The tips of his fingers pressed into each socket as he rubbed his eyes. Battling the addiction was hard when one had the fortitude and support of others close at hand to keep him in check. He had neither. At that moment, he regretted walking down the path he had—drinking and all.

Russell lifted his head, then glanced out of the window to the darkness beyond the glass panes. The murk seemed hollow; empty and vast. It was odd not to see any sort of light or hint of civilization.

He spotted movement in front of the house, or so he thought. He squinted, then opened his eyes. There was nothing there. It could've been an animal passing through or just his imagination. They were in the mountains, after all.

The porch creaked. Russell froze. He didn't imagine that. He tilted his head to the side and listened.

The boards creaked again, then stopped. Something was out there, skulking about close to the house. If that was an animal, it was being more curious than Russell figured it should be.

Was the front door locked down? Russell couldn't remember if Cathy had checked it before heading off to bed. This was her place, and she knew how to secure her own house. Still, the thought remained.

Russell skirted around the kitchen table. He hugged the wall in the direction of the front door, listening for any additional warnings.

Cathy hadn't stirred, nor Max.

The flickering from the flame cast shadows along the walls, which added to the eerie ambiance. Each step Russell took made his heart pound harder. He gulped the lump in his throat and stopped shy of the entrance to the cabin.

He craned his neck and peered through the window. From his vantage point, it was difficult to make anything out. He couldn't spot any movement, but that didn't mean there wasn't anyone there.

Russell leaned forward a bit more and looked out the sides of the window. Glass shattered from the kitchen, stealing his attention away from the entrance. Something dense hammered the floor and rolled over the wooden planks.

What the hell?

Max barked from the other room, and clawed at the door, fighting to get out.

A bottle came hurtling through the busted window. The tip was ablaze and glowed a fiery orange. It took a second for Russell to figure out what it was.

The Molotov cocktail shattered on the floor. A fiery glow blossomed as is spread across the wood. The crackling of flames consuming the house played in his ears. Smoke tainted the air.

Russell covered his mouth and swatted at the smoke.

Cathy and Max barreled out of her bedroom in a dead sprint. A look of shock and bewilderment filled her gaze. The fire consumed everything in its path and continued chewing through the rest of the cabin.

The front door exploded open just as Russell stepped away to combat the raging inferno. The jamb splintered and the window shattered into a million fine pieces.

Russell flinched and covered his head with his arms. He turned toward the porch, confused as to what was happening. Shards of glass crunched under his boots.

Under the cloak of night, a figure dressed in a green camo raincoat rushed headlong inside the cabin. He paused for a blink before setting his sights on Russell. He took a step back as if surprised to find Russell there.

His face was covered with a ski mask. Only his eyes and the stray hairs from his mustache and beard were visible.

Russell balled his fingers into fists and gnashed his teeth. He charged the intruder. The two men collided and pushed out onto the porch while throwing punches at one another.

The man in the raincoat was strong. His heavy hand pummeled the side of Russell's face. Russell deflected the man's arm and jabbed him square in the nose—a lighting fast strike that sent the man stumbling backward.

Both of his hands palmed his bleeding nose as he grumbled in pain. Russell punched him in the gut, then finished him off with an uppercut. His head snapped backward in a blink, and he crumbled to the ground.

Russell stood over the defeated man for a second, making sure he was no longer a threat.

Max barked from the interior of the cabin which was trumped by the loud, raging fire feeding on the log house. Russell peered back to the inferno that burned unchallenged. He ran toward the entrance as thick, white smoke escaped from the opening.

Max materialized from the dense cloud. He leapt from the porch and hit the ground running. Cathy stumbled out of the cabin with a rucksack fixed in her hand, and a rifle slung over her shoulder.

She dropped to her knees at the edge of the porch. The palm of her hand covered her nose and mouth. She hacked and coughed, struggling to breathe.

Fiery tendrils crawled out of the windows and over the exterior of the cabin. The heat from the blaze felt like a thousand suns against Russell's skin. It grew more intense with each second they stood there. He squinted and shielded his face from the torrid hellfire as he grabbed Cathy's arm.

"Come on, we need to move away from here," Russell lifted Cathy to her feet and helped her off the porch. The man in the raincoat was gone. He had vanished without a trace.

That didn't matter now. They had bigger problems facing them.

Max barked at the log house without pause. He'd pace back and forth, then rear back on his hind legs while howling.

Both Russell and Cathy collapsed to the grass. They were far enough away from the fire to be out of harm's way. A wheeze escaped her lips as she struggled to breath. Russell coughed and hacked, trying to expel the smoke that had a tight grip on his lungs.

"Are you—ok?" he asked through a coughing fit.

Cathy's face was smirched with soot. Her eyes shined as tears streamed over her soiled cheeks. "Yeah. I'm fine."

Russell placed his hand on her shoulder as Max trotted over to her side. He licked at the sadness that raced down the sides of her face as she rubbed the crown of his head.

Off in the distance, Russell spotted two glowing red lights, followed by the squealing of tires.

Bastards.

He stood up and dashed around the cabin toward the driveway that led to the street. The building that housed Cathy's Jeep and other tools was ablaze as well.

Russell stopped on a dime and slid over the loose dirt. His chin dropped as he watched the flames consume the building. He turned on the heels of his boots, searching the darkness for a watering hose, or anything else he could use to douse the fire.

Cathy rushed over to Russell with Max matching her stride for stride. She peered at the fire with an emotionless gaze. Her eyes shined with sadness, but Cathy didn't break down. She ran her hand under her nose and cleared her throat. The torment of losing her house and valuables fell to the wayside. She grabbed Russell's arm and tugged.

"It's not safe to be around here." Her voice was infused with anger. It sounded like a hoarse growl.

"What about the fires?" Russell countered while pointing at the blazing inferno. "We need to put them out."

Cathy shook her head while she jerked at his arm. "It's too far gone. We couldn't put it out even if we wanted to. Besides, there's combustible materials in the garage as well as the house. It could blow at any minute."

She secured the strap to the rucksack around her waist and adjusted the rifle on her shoulder. Clutched in her hand was a small, black tactical flashlight.

Russell glanced at the garage. The flames danced in his eyes as his ticket to getting back to Sarah evaporated. Meager shreds of hope remained. The same anger that surged in Cathy had now spawned life in Russell as he back-peddled away.

Max took point with Cathy and Russell flanking him. She thumbed the switch to the flashlight. A strident beam of light shot from the lens and illuminated the uneven terrain before them.

They darted past the tree line at full tilt and entered the thicket. The sharp, pointed ends of the bushes stabbed at their bodies as they forced their way through.

An explosion went off.

The ground quaked under their feet.

A large fireball arched into the darkness and blossomed at the peak.

They dropped to the dirt and shielded their heads with their arms.

Max cowered next to Cathy as she held him close.

Russell stayed by their side as he braced for the unknown.

A slight ringing festered inside his ears. It made it hard to hear over the crackling of the fire and smaller, less volatile explosions that popped off.

Cathy removed her arms, then stood up. Russell followed suit, although, he was a bit more apprehensive and moved at a slower pace.

"You good," Russell asked panting.

Cathy bowed her head. Coils of flames arched from the fire and brimstone, lashing across the night sky.

She looked to the road and narrowed her gaze. A scowl washed over her unkempt face. Her brow furrowed in anger as her nostrils flared.

Russell could relate. Having someone rob one of their life was never an easy pill to swallow. One would want nothing more than payback. Revenge for what had been taken from them.

Cathy turned away from the fire and patted her leg. Max snapped to and waited for her command. "Let's get moving."

Russell glanced at Cathy, who had walked away with Max by her side, then back to the dying remnants of her house. "Where are we going?"

"To see a friend."

CHAPTER NINETEEN

SARAH

The city was in a state of turmoil. Pandemonium reigned over the inhabitants like a heavy-handed dictator and hadn't let up. It was scary to see the madness unfold during the day, but the unhinged metropolis was just as unsettling at night.

An endless ether of darkness swept across the city like a cover had been draped over it. Smoke swallowed the moon and stars. The only visible light was from the orange, fiery glow of buildings burning in the not too far distance.

A burnt smell tainted the air. It clung to Sarah's skin and clothes like a leech. It made her sick to her stomach, but she held firm and pushed through the unsettling sensation.

Boston looked like a third-world country that was in the throes of war. The lack of lights from the buildings and streetlamps made it feel desolate and abandoned.

Society had crumbled and reverted to a primitive state faster than Sarah thought possible. With any such cataclysmic event, she had thought it might take a few weeks before people regressed to baser instincts, but with the power gone and no communications, it happened in a blink.

It was like a switch was thrown and anarchy was now the rule of law. Not all joined the depraved in causing havoc, but enough had.

In the end, though, it wasn't that farfetched. At any given moment, anyone could see that humanity teetered on the edge of a full-blown volcanic meltdown. They just needed a reason, a catalyst to kick things off.

Black Friday shopping was a prime example. Those steep discounts churned the waters of the population like chum to sharks. Once the doors opened, and the flood of people rushed in, it was every man and woman for themselves. This was no different.

That simple and yet scary notion was part of the reason why Sarah wanted to find Mandy as fast as possible. Out of all the people in Boston, Mandy was her best friend, and closest confidant. When her life went to hell a year ago, Mandy helped her through the pain when Russell was emotionally unable to do so. Because of that, Sarah had to find her, and get off the streets until they could figure out what was going on, and what they're next move would be.

Mandy's apartment was on the other side of town from where Sarah was. She figured that's where Mandy would've headed when the shit hit the fan. No doubt, Copley Place would've been closed down, or worse yet, a free-for-all for the looters and scum looking to take advantage of the discord. Given the state of the city, making it to Mandy's, or home for that matter, at night, was not going to be the best move.

Powerless World

Sarah checked her phone for a signal, hoping at least communications had been restored. Service was still suspended and displayed the zero with a line through it. Her battery was desperately low and needed to be charged, but that was going to be easier said than done.

Crap.

Her shoulders sagged as she sighed in frustration. Sarah continued on through the blinding city, alone and on edge, looking for a place that she could hold up until daybreak.

The Glock stayed glued to her hand with her finger over the kill switch. Her head was on a constant swivel from the ominous sounds that loomed from the shadows of the buildings and alleyways.

There weren't as many people out as there were when the sun was high in the sky. Some of the ones who were out had flashlights that sliced through the blackness as they flew past her.

Ghastly gray figures stalked the streets, weaving in and out of the pockets of cars that sat abandoned on the roads. Sarah kept a keen eye on the cloaked figures who looked more like demons lurking in the darkness than people.

Glass shattered.

The shadowy figures leaned through the missing windows. Jagged pieces of glass rimmed the outside. They rummaged through the vehicles left behind without regard. Beams of light illuminated the vehicles and the criminals ransacking them.

Footfalls echoed behind Sarah. Each fell in sync with hers. She tilted her head to the side, and tried to lay eyes on who was trailing her. All she could see was a black figure, his identity protected by the night.

The Creeper popped into her head with his evil grin that he showed when dubious intentions were on his mind.

A wave of panic crashed into Sarah as she picked up the pace. The man flanking her responded in kind. She looked to the brick buildings that lined both sides of the road. The windows were dark and void of any light. She was on her own, and would have to defend herself as best she could if it came to that.

The footfalls increased to a sprint that gained on Sarah. She stopped, then turned around to face her attacker. The Glock lifted up with both hands clutching the grip. If he was searching for an easy mark, he'd soon regret his choice.

The man rushed past her. He didn't stop or try to engage Sarah in any sort of way. He peered back over his shoulder as panicked breaths escaped his lips.

Christ.

Sarah breathed heavily as she watched the man race down the sidewalk to the intersection. He vanished around the corner of the building without slowing his hastened pace.

Although Sarah had found strength in herself over the past year, a part of her wished Russell was by her side. Despite his flaws and inability to deal with the death of their daughter, she knew he'd protect her at any cost.

Trudging through the darkness of the powerless city, and dealing with the criminal element that lurked around every corner, made Sarah want Russell back that much more. It wasn't just because she was scared from the threats the world had to offer, and she needed him to protect her.

She missed the comfort she once had with him, and how he made her feel like a queen. The love that they shared, and the deep bond that kept them tethered to each other. Although she had distanced herself from him, because of how he was behaving, she still wanted him back, and hoped she could tell him as much.

Powerless World

Gunfire crackled in the dismal sky. It was close. The looters ransacking the vehicles stopped, then stepped away from the cars.

Their flashlights trained down the street from whence Sarah had come. They surveyed the sidewalks and the few cars that were parked askew in the road.

A set of headlights slashed through the darkness and shined their way. The grumbling of an engine echoed down the street as the lights grew larger, and more intense.

The looters fled from sight with what valuables they had scored. They scurried like mice back to the shadows of the buildings and alleyways.

Sarah gulped. The looters were afraid of whatever it was that was heading their way. She figured it wasn't the police from the absence of flashing red and blue lights.

No. It had to be something more sinister to cause the dreadful hoodlums to flee in fear.

The car skirted around the vehicles in the road. Music blared from the windows. Sarah backpedaled as the car hopped up on the sidewalk. It straddled the road and walkway, bypassing the pocket of cars that blocked the street.

Sarah turned and hoofed it down the sidewalk to the corner of the building. She skirted the edge, and continued running at a dead sprint.

The vehicle's engine grew louder as did the music. She had seen numerous cars and other vehicles plow over sidewalks and run over any pedestrians who got in their way. Sarah wasn't sure who they were, or what they were after, but she didn't want to find out. It was better to play on the side of caution.

Derek Shupert

Her feet hammered the concrete as she searched for a building to slip into. At this point, it didn't matter. Anything would do until the car went about its way.

She rushed past a sprawling apartment complex and stopped. At the top of the landing was a single door. She jerked her chin back to the intersection. The width of the beam from the car's headlights grew larger. It was now or never.

Sarah tromped up the stairs and hit the landing. She grabbed the handle to the door and pulled, but it didn't budge. She tried again, only to get the same result.

Darkness filled her gaze through the thick-panned window. Sarah squinted while tugging on the handle in search of any movement inside.

Her fists pounded the rigid, painted surface of the door as she watched the intersection. The squealing of tires and the loud music made Sarah panic as the car materialized from the corner of the building. It continued over the sidewalk and onto the street in her direction.

A light from inside the building blasted Sarah in the face. Her hands sprung up in front of her as she took a step back. The door swung open and grazed her fingers. Inside the hall stood a tall, slender man wielding a pistol. He trained the barrel at Sarah as she diverted her gaze.

"Please, don't shoot," she pleaded.

The man craned his neck and glanced down to the street as the car rolled into view. He thumbed the switch to the flashlight he held, then waved his arm.

"Hurry up. Get inside," his voice boomed with urgency.

Sarah slipped past the agitated man in a blink and ran into the building. He grabbed the edge of the door and slammed it as the car drove past the building.

Powerless World

He secured the lock to the door and stood off to the side of the entrance while staring out of the window. Not a single word was spoken as he held the pistol in the air.

The loud music dissipated and faded away, bringing a wave of relief to Sarah. She sighed, then deflated against the wall. "Thank you for letting me in."

The man thumbed the switch to the flashlight which lit up the dark hall. "No problem. Looks like they've moved on. It's not safe out there right now."

Sarah took a deep breath, then exhaled. She kept a close eye on the stranger. Her hand stayed near the Glock. "That's an understatement. I thought it was bad during the day, but without the lights, the night has proven to be much worse. I don't feel safe out there with everything that is happening."

The man looked at Sarah and nodded. "Yeah. There are some real dirtbags taking advantage of the power outage. I've seen some pretty bad things happen since all this started. That's why I'm on edge and reluctant to let anyone in here. Hard to tell who's a threat and who isn't."

"Do I look like a threat?" Sarah posed.

He glanced at the Glock she had in her hand. "That piece you're holding kind of says that you are. But, given how you were banging on that door and all, I figured you were more worried about whoever was in that car than anything else."

"I don't know who they are. People have gone crazy out there. Doing horrible, dreadful things amidst the chaos, so I'm a bit on edge."

The man tilted his head, then secured his piece within the waistband of his denim jeans. "I can understand that. You can hang out here until morning, if you like."

Sarah looked past the slender man and through the window to the world beyond the building. She wasn't keen on venturing back out there at the moment. Not with the surly types scouring the city streets for an easy target. She didn't trust this man, but he seemed to be the lesser of two evils.

"Thanks. That's much appreciated," she said. "Just to let you know, though, I'm not giving up my Glock. And if you think or hint at trying to do something, I'll have no problem shooting you."

He held his hands in the air and bowed his head. "Duly noted and understood. The name is Rick Stone, by the way."

"Sarah Cage."

CHAPTER TWENTY

RUSSELL

Life had a funny way of kicking a man when he was down. Like a heavy boot crushing his throat, Russell felt the squeeze. That's what it seemed like, anyway.

Within a day, things had turned from all right to a complete crap storm, one he couldn't escape or stop from happening. No matter what he did or tried, life was out to get him. Russell had to remind himself that although things were bleak, he was still alive. He had that to be thankful for.

Cathy was silent. Losing her house and valuables pissed her off. She didn't have to say as much for Russell to figure that out. She stomped through the woods like a woman on a mission. Her shoulders didn't sag with sadness or defeat. No whimpers fled her lips that Russell could hear, which spoke volumes of how tough and resilient she was.

Russell couldn't blame her. He was pissed as well. Not only did they take the house from Cathy, but they had put reaching her daughter and Sarah at risk. It was an act he couldn't let slide.

Max had taken point a few paces ahead of Cathy. His nose trained to the crunchy leaves that carpeted the forest floor. He'd rummage through the small mounds, in search of whatever scent or noise tickled his curiosity.

The grumble of thunder rumbled in the distance.

Cathy looked at the canopy of trees above them. "Sounds like we have a storm rolling in."

Russell glanced at the black sky. It was difficult to see through the umbrella of vegetation that hung over them. He craned his neck, but couldn't pierce the dark veil of branches and leaves. "How far away do you think it is?"

"Not too far. We should be to Thomas's cabin before it really gets going, though."

Max paused. He lowered his head and stared at the steep ridge before him.

Cathy flanked him. She craned her neck and shined the light down the slope.

"Problem?" Russell inquired.

She shook her head while sweeping the area from side to side. "No. Just trying to find a safe way down, is all."

Russell peered at the trees and rocks that were nestled within the verdure along the slope. He couldn't find a way down that didn't elevate their risk for injury. It was hard to gauge the terrain with the darkness that covered the area like a blanket. Only the vague outline of the rocks and trees caught his eye, which wasn't too helpful. His ankle was doing better, but it was still sore, and could pose an issue if he tweaked it the wrong way.

Cathy patted Max's right side twice.

Powerless World

He turned in the direction of her gesture and continued on. Slow and steady, Max traversed the slope. He made short work of the steep incline.

When he reached the bottom, Max glanced to the ridge and barked. He sat on his haunches and waited for his handler to arrive.

Cathy shined the light to the path that snaked to the base of the ground where Max was, then peered at Russell. "Take it slow and mimic what I do. It's not that bad if you're careful and watch your footing. Just don't rush it. If you slip and fall, you're going to take me down with you."

"Did you want me to wait till you reach the bottom?"

Cathy shook her head. "I'd rather not. How are you going to be able to see where you're stepping if you did? I don't have another flashlight. I had this one stowed in my bug out pack."

Russell patted his back pocket where his phone was. "I can use the flashlight from my phone if I need to."

Cathy snickered. "I guarantee that flashlight on your phone isn't near as bright as my Maglite. Besides, you slip and lose your grip on it, well, you might as well kiss it good bye. It'll be harder than hell to locate it in that thicket, or it'll break on any of those boulders down there. It's your call, though."

She was right. Her Maglite's beam was intense, and lit up the ground without much effort. Russell doubted his phone could do better. Plus, he didn't want to take the chance of breaking or losing it. It was worthless at the moment, but cell service could be returned at any time, and he wanted to be ready to dial Sarah.

Russell pointed at the slope. "I'll just follow you down. Shouldn't be a problem."

Cathy trained the light at the ground. The large, circular beam washed over the rocks and grass that coated the stair-like steps within the earth.

Much like Max, Cathy navigated the face of the hill without fault. She paused about halfway down, then turned back to Russell who was a bit·more apprehensive.

"You coming?" she called out. "The longer we take, the more likely we are to get rained on. It gets cold out here, and being wet won't make it any better."

"Yeah." Russell sucked in a gulp of air, then released it through pursed lips. The last thing he wanted was to be cold and wet. It was already chilly. The brisk wind nipped at his flesh and tried to penetrate his clothes.

Max barked, then groaned. He was getting impatient. Russell couldn't see him, but he could hear the anxious dog moving about.

Russell eased down the uneven slope, one precarious step after another. Cathy got back on the move, and they worked their way down to the base.

Cathy shined the light on Max. He was on his feet, ready to move. She rubbed the crown of his head as he stretched to meet her hand. His tongue hung from the side of his snout, and he groaned at her touch.

"All right. Come on. Let's go see Thomas."

Bark.

Max trotted away. Cathy and Russell flanked his wagging tail as he led them through a clearing.

Clapping thunder shook the ground. Strident white lines of lightning slithered across the puffy clouds like veins. The whistling of wind blowing through the branches accompanied the incoming storm.

Cathy paid the weather no mind. She kept trudging through the clearing to the tree line ahead of them.

Russell was glad she knew where she was going. He was lost within the tress and thickets.

Powerless World

A guiding light in the distance caught Russell's eye as rain trickled from the heavens and splashed against him. A shiver slid down his body as the flannel shirt he wore soaked in the moisture.

Cathy pulled the hood of her coat up over her head, then wrapped her arms over her chest as she scaled the side of the hill. Max stopped and gave his body a good shake, freeing the fur of the rain.

"See. We almost made it before it really got going," Cathy said as she glanced to Russell.

Beads of rain raced down the sides of Russell's face. Another shiver overtook him as his teeth chattered. "This guy isn't going to mind us just stopping by in the middle of the night unannounced, is he?"

Cathy ducked and moved in a wide arch around a tree that had limbs reaching toward the ground. Her boots sloshed through the carpet of soggy leaves as she made her way back toward Russell. "He shouldn't. It's been a while since I've been over to visit with him, though. Thomas lives alone and doesn't get out much. Can't remember the last time he went to town either. He doesn't care for most folks."

Sounds like he's going to be super excited to see us, then, Russell thought.

The rain picked up. Another spate of lightning crackled in the sky overhead, illuminating the swollen clouds. Heavy thunder rumbled through the mountains.

Max galloped up the hill toward the front of the house. The lights in the windows evaporated, casting the large dwelling in darkness.

Cathy paused. She whistled for Max who stopped, then peered back toward them. His ears stood on end and twitched as he trotted back to her side.

"What is it?" Russell inquired.

The beam from the Maglite brushed over the front of the house. Cathy swept the porch from one side to the other as if she had reservations about going any farther. "It's probably nothing. Just got a funny feeling is all."

Rain saturated Russell's hair and the flannel shirt he had on. The slight shiver he was battling had turned to convulsions of cold. "Can we at least get under the porch and out of the rain until we hash this out?"

Max gave his matted fur another shake as Cathy looked at the house.

"Yeah. Come on. I'm probably still rattled from what happened earlier." Cathy pulled at the strap of her rifle that hung from her shoulder as they continued on toward the house. She didn't remove it, but the simple tug at the weapon made Russell take notice.

"You're not expecting trouble, are you?"

"I wasn't expecting the sort of trouble we got back at my place, but here we are." Her tone was laced with indignation. "Like I said, I imagine everything's fine. Just being cautious is all."

Max growled and lowered his ears. The damp fur along the ridge of his spine stood on end. Something had gotten his attention.

Cathy stopped at his side and took a knee. "What is it?"

A rustling noise from the west side of the house triggered a bark, then another growl. Max took off at a gallop and tore around the side of the house, vanishing from sight.

"Damn it," Cathy groused. "It's probably just a coon or something."

She ran after him through the sheets of rain. Russell booked it to the entrance of the house, splashing through the soggy grass as he leapt up onto the porch.

His hand ran over his face and wiped away the wetness that covered his skin. The flannel shirt clung to his shuddering frame. His jeans were soaked through. The only part of his body that wasn't wet were his feet. The boots did a good job of keeping the rain at bay.

Russell ran his hand through his hair as he looked down either side of the porch. There was no sign of Cathy or Max, just the endless abyss of night and the skeletal limbs that reached out like boney demons.

The rain pelting the sheet metal covering overhead was loud and obtrusive, and made it difficult to hear.

Another wave of thunder exploded. Russell flinched, then turned to the angry sky.

A sense of dread washed over Russell as if the reaper was whispering in his ear. He shook off the uneasy sensation as best he could, and faced the window next to the front door.

The interior of the house was pitch black. Russell squinted and peered through the glass. Lightning thrashed the dreary sky without pause. The brief flashes offered a snapshot of the interior before it went dark.

Russell couldn't spot any movement in the second or two of light, which was strange. The lights were on mere moments ago, but he could've gone to bed.

What if something had happened to the old man? He didn't know Thomas's age, or anything about him for that matter, but he was older and could've experienced a stroke or some other life-threatening affliction.

Worse yet, what if someone had broken into his house, and snuffed him? Maybe Marcus sent his goons over here to tune the old man up for whatever reason. Russell was a bit out of his depth in trying to figure out Marcus and his relationship with everyone else, but given what his thugs did to Cathy, and Russell, he knew enough to know Marcus was a piece of crap.

The faint hint of a bark battled the elements. Russell stepped away from the window and searched for Max. He craned his neck and lifted up on the tips of his toes. More barks sounded off, but Russell couldn't spot Max or Cathy.

The uncertainty of the situation he was in compounded on Russell's mind. He paced about the porch, trying to figure out what his next move should be.

The front door to the house was open. He hadn't noticed that it was. A figure stalked the darkness that clung to the interior of the home. It didn't look like a grown man. No. It was much shorter and closer to the ground.

Trepidation clawed at Russell's nerves as he backed away from the entrance of the house. He stepped down from the porch into the furor. Something didn't feel right.

The shadowy figure rushed out of the house—a blur of black. Instincts took hold. Russell's hands came up as the growling creature leapt from the porch.

The two collided. The bulk of the growling and vicious animal knocked Russell hard to the ground. Sharp teeth glistened with every bolt of lightning that slithered along the clouds.

Russell grabbed the dog by the throat, fighting to keep the animal away. Bright, yellow eyes narrowed as the tepid breath from the animal's snout blasted his face.

Max materialized from the ether beyond the west side of the house at a dead sprint. Barking and growling, he bore down on the animal that had Russell pinned to the ground.

The dog pressed forward, digging its paws into the grass and mud as it snapped at Russell's face. Max jumped and tackled the beast.

Powerless World

Both animals rolled over the grass, each snapping and clawing at the other. Cathy hammered the soggy ground as she rushed to Russell's aid.

A gunshot erupted from the porch. The sharp report of the thunderous canon snared everyone's attention. Cathy wrenched Russell off the ground as both dogs continued their heated strife.

"Butch. Come," an old, gruff voice barked over the rain.

The dog broke away from Max, and rushed to his handlers' side. Max trotted over to Cathy and Russell who stared down the barrel of a shotgun.

"Thomas?" Cathy called out.

"Who the hell is asking?" the old man yelled back.

"It's Cathy and Max."

Thomas fumbled with the side of his leg, searching the pockets of his pants for his flashlight. The large, menacing dog stood obediently by Thomas's side. He sat on his haunches and watched the trio with a vigilant gaze.

Russell had grown tired of animals attacking him. He'd had his fair share of the dangerous creatures.

The double-barrel shotgun remained fixed in their direction as the old man thumbed the light to the flashlight he wielded. The bright gleam blared from the lens and shined over their drenched faces.

Cathy pulled the hood of her coat back and shielded her face.

"Jesus Christ, Cathy." Thomas's rigid demeanor vanished in a blink as he lowered the gun. He trained the barrel at the ground. "What the hell are you and Max doing out here during this squall? I could've shot you."

"It's a long story. Can we come in, and I'll fill you in?"

"Of course. Yeah." Thomas waved his hand and turned to the side, motioning for them to enter his dwelling.

153

Butch remained by his side as Cathy and the others ran toward the porch. He growled at the sight of them, revealing his teeth at the unfamiliar guest.

Max responded in much the same manner as he flanked Cathy and trailed her inside the home.

Russell stared at the large beast, and made a wide arch around the golden-eyed protector. The dog didn't budge from Thomas's side. His head turned and followed Russell's movement as he darted inside the house.

Thomas retreated with Butch into the log building. The dog shook the water free of its coat in the entryway as his handler leaned the double-barrel shotgun against the wall.

"That's one hell of a downpour out there," Thomas groused.

His agitated tone reminded Russell of his grandfather who always sounded like he was pissed off and irritated at the world.

Thomas slammed the door shut, then removed the coat he wore. Butch watched Russell and the others in the dark. His gaze focused on their every move—a sentry for the older man.

Each step Thomas took looked unsteady, as if his legs weren't cooperating. He'd pause, then lean against the wall. "Damn weather has the joints of my knees stiff as a board. Makes it hard to function."

Light from across the room grew. Cathy stood near a lantern that rested on top a small, wooden table. The soft-white glow illuminated a portion of the living space which was cluttered with copious amounts of furniture and knickknacks.

"We really appreciate you letting us in," Cathy said. "I wasn't sure where else to go. I would've called ahead, but the phones aren't working."

Thomas dismissed her words with a flick of his wrist. "No need to thank me, dear. I'm just sorry about pulling the double barrel out on you. Thought I had some trespassers trolling my property. I can't stand that. Irritates the fire out of me."

He tracked past the front door to the dark cherry console table that was under the window. Simple grunts of discomfort fled his lips as he bent down to retrieve another lantern that was on the bottom shelf.

Cathy removed her coat and folded it over her arm. A portion of her hair was wet. She ran her fingers through the damp strands, then flicked the water free of her hand.

Russell shivered in the middle of the room, unable to stop the convulsing of his limbs. His hands rubbed up and down his arms, trying to warm them.

"Mind if I make a fire, Thomas?" Cathy inquired.

"Knock yourself out. Should be plenty of wood over there."

Thomas sat the old, reddish-brown lantern on top of the console table and turned it on, adding more light to the home. It looked like a kerosene lamp which had been repurposed in a way that kept it from having to be lit with a match.

He set the lamp in the middle of the table, then turned toward Russell. "Best fifteen dollars I ever spent. Solar-powered lanterns repurposed from some old kerosene ones I had sitting out in my garage."

"That's pretty ingenious," Russell stuttered through chattering teeth. He extended his trembling hand out. "I'm Russell Cage, by the way. Your hospitality is appreciated, sir."

"Sir?" the old man belted. "Hot damn, Cathy. Did you hear that? Seems like you found a respectable man here. Thomas Kinkade. Nice to meet you, son."

Russell lowered his head.

Cathy shook her head. "It's not like that, Thomas. He's just a friend I'm helping out."

Cathy eyed Russell and blushed. She cleared her throat, then looked away. He understood where she was coming from. Keep it short, sweet, and on point. Besides, he didn't view Cathy that way, either.

"Aw, hell. Friends or not, I'm just glad to see you hanging out with someone other than that four-legged pup you got over there."

Max was seated in front of the fireplace as Cathy piled wood on the hearth.

Cathy pointed to the black dog that stood at Thomas's side. "When did you get the dog? It's a cane corso, right?"

Thomas rubbed the top of the brute's head. His fingers scratched behind the dog's cropped ears. The dog licked at his fingers, then ran his large, pink tongue around the ridge of his snout.

"Yeah. It is. I got Butch a few weeks back from a friend of mine. They're great guard dogs. Protective and efficient at tracking. Figured it would be good to have an extra set of eyes and ears being so far out. I'm not getting any younger, that's for damn sure. He trained Butch well."

Russell dipped his chin and looked at the stout dog, who was calm and at ease—though, Russell knew that could change within a blink if need be.

"He is intimidating, that's for sure," Russell said while keeping his distance.

Butch panted with his tongue hanging from his snout. He stood up and gave his coat another shake. Water slung from his fur in all directions.

"He can be, but he's a great dog." Thomas looked at Russell. "Sorry again for siccing him on you. All I saw was a light outside in the rain and some dark figures. Spooked me a bit. Max is all right, isn't he?"

"He's fine," Cathy responded as she got the fire going. "That isn't the worst scrap he's ever been in."

Max groaned from the rug that sat in front of the fireplace.

"Oh, good. He's still my good boy," Thomas said.

Russell held up his hand. "I guess we kind of asked for it. I don't blame you in the least. You're way up here in the mountains during a storm at night, and you spy some people walking around outside of your house that you weren't expecting. Hell, after what we've been through at her place, having the guard dogs seems like a must."

Thomas staggered around the furniture with Butch flanking him. The dog approached Max as the two sniffed each other. "What happened at your place? It doesn't have to do with that fire that I saw a bit ago, does it? That orange glow would have been hard to miss."

Russell moved around the couch to the fireplace to get warm, and to dry off.

Cathy poked at the logs as the old man took a seat in a wooden rocking chair across from her. "That's actually why we're here."

Derek Shupert

CHAPTER TWENTY-ONE

SARAH

Sleep with one eye open and a finger over the trigger.

It was a simple phrase Sarah told herself while sitting on the chair in Rick's apartment, just in case she nodded off.

A few candles had been lit and placed around the dwelling. It added a warm glow to the otherwise sparse living space. Slouched in the brown leather rocking chair, Sarah fought the urge to drift off.

The day's events had taken their toll. She had been rung through the ringer with no end in sight. Her mind jumped through the numerous frantic thoughts that plagued her.

Death.

Chaos.

Mandy's whereabouts.

How Russell was doing.

She hoped he was all right, and that she'd be able to see him again soon. There were so many things she wanted to say. To tell him how she really felt. The thought of not being able to do so made her sad and regret how curt and cold she was to him when they last spoke. Given how things were, though, that seemed to be a stretch since she didn't even know where he was.

Rick was a sentry, standing guard at the window that looked over the street in front of the apartment building. He had been planted there for a while.

Sarah couldn't remember how long. It seemed irrelevant. The only time he had stepped away from the window was to get her some water, and whatever dry food he had in his pantry.

She snacked on some junk food which her stomach appreciated. Chips, crackers, and some powered donuts. Not the most nutritious meal, but it was better than nothing.

He glanced at her every so often with a stern and rigid gaze. Focus filled his face. He was on guard from the threats that loomed beyond his walls.

The Glock rested in Sarah's lap with her hand clutching the grip. She watched his every move. Trust was a valuable commodity for her, and it had to be earned. It wasn't given away without thought now. Rick seemed like a nice enough person, but that could change without warning, and she had to be ready.

"Have you gotten enough to eat?" Rick inquired while leaning against the narrow piece of wall between the two bay windows. "I've got more food in there. I had just gone to the store before all this happened."

Her stomach was content at the moment. She didn't see the need to gorge herself on food just because. Stress eating was never a good thing.

She shook her head, then rubbed her hand over her long, tired face. "I'm good, for now. Thank you."

Powerless World

Rick scratched at the stubble on the side of his chin. "If you get hungry later, you can help yourself. I don't mind."

Noises from the hallway drifted into the tiny apartment. Raised voices bickered. Doors slammed. Heavy footsteps tromped along the floors above and down the hall.

People were on edge—scared from whatever had happened. The tumult that called out from all around confirmed that.

Sarah nodded toward the hallway where some of the rantings were taking place. "Your neighbors seem nice and friendly. Are they always so vocal?"

Rick turned toward the door that led into his apartment, then rolled his eyes. "Some, yes. There are a few couples here who act like dogs and cats that are forced to coexist. I think the others are just worried. They're all good people here. The ones I know, anyway. It just doesn't help when you have low lifes and thugs running rampant on the streets and causing problems for everyone. It just adds more stress to an already stressful situation."

She glanced at the door and listened to the muffled yells and arguments that reminded her of spats with Russell. They'd had some epic ones for sure.

"Do you know what happened, by chance?" she posed. "What caused the blackout?"

He shrugged, then folded his arms across his chest. "No clue. I've heard numerous rumors from my neighbors who think they know what happened, but I'm doubtful."

"Oh? Such as?" Her brow raised in curiosity.

"I'll spare you the details, but the most outlandish theory swimming around this place is, I can't even believe I'm about to say this, aliens."

"Aliens, huh?" Sarah said. "I've heard people say something about an EMP attack or a similar event, but nothing about aliens. I'm kind of skeptical about that."

"What? You don't believe in little green men arriving in spaceships and all that nonsense?" His tone was sarcastic at best.

"Not really. I rank that up with sightings of bigfoot and the Loch Ness Monster."

Rick agreed with a nod of his head. "Yeah. I'd rank that up there with those as well. Seems fitting."

"I did hear a few people think it was some sort of a nuclear attack or a bomb that took out the power grid. The North Koreans seem to get thrown to the front of the line. The usual suspects, I guess. That or ISIS, I suppose."

A bright light shone in through the window where Rick was standing. He leaned toward the glass, and craned his neck, searching for the source.

A loud thumping sound approached the complex. It grew louder the closer it got.

"Well, it definitely wasn't an EMP. I can tell you that much," Rick said.

"EMP?" Sarah parroted. "I'm not following."

Rick didn't take his eyes off the window as he hunted for what sounded like a helicopter buzzing around the city.

"Electromagnetic Pulse," he clarified. "That will destroy pretty much anything that's electronic. Cars, aircraft, your phone, appliances, etc. Since that chopper is flying over the city, an EMP blast is out of the question. But something similar had to happen for everything to just go out like it did."

Sarah got off the couch. It was making her sluggish and sleepy. She needed the rest, but didn't feel comfortable doing so around Rick.

She skirted some of the boxes he had stacked throughout his living room. It was hard to tell if he had just moved in or was too lazy to unpack his belongings.

He crouched, then pointed to the black sky overhead. "I think it went over us and kept going."

The noise from the chopper had dissipated some, but she could still hear it. Sarah pressed the side of her face to the window and looked for the spotlight. "I can't see it."

Rick turned toward the entryway of his abode. "Come on. We might be able to get a better feel of everything from the roof."

"Is it even unlocked?"

He shrugged. "If it isn't, then we'll unlock it. I'd like to get a sense of what the rest of the city looks like."

Sarah didn't need to go to the roof to know that things were bad. The panic and straight fear of the unknown had latched onto the populous like a parasite.

However, getting the lay of the land from an elevated position would allow her to gauge how Boston was doing overall.

"Lead the way."

Rick pulled the pistol from his waistband and chambered a round. It looked like her Glock 43, only bigger.

"Do you think we'll have a problem out there where we'll need our guns," she inquired as she flanked him to the door of his apartment.

"I don't think so, but I'd rather play on the side of caution than not bring my Glock with me. For the most part, it goes where I go." He stopped at a waist-high table next to the door. A flashlight sat face down on the surface. He secured the Glock in his waistband and grabbed the flashlight.

Sarah wasn't comfortable enough to do the same. She felt more secure having the weapon at the ready.

"Are you a cop or something?" Sarah asked.

The notion pulled a snicker from Rick as he shook his head. "Lord, no. Why do you ask?"

"I don't know. You just seem like you're standing guard over the building, is all. Made me think you were a cop or some kind of law enforcement officer," Sarah said.

Rick thumbed the switch to the light. A strident beam of white sprung from the lens as he turned to face her. "I did run a PI firm for a spell before it went belly up and took most of my savings with it. That's part of the reason why I live in this spacious paradise. I was downstairs to keep an eye on things because the last thing anyone wants is to have a bunch of opportunistic hoodlums get into the building and cause a bunch of problems. The police are stretched thin, and any sort of robberies or other violent crimes aren't going to be responded to in a timely manner, if at all. Our best defense against any threats is going to be ourselves until order is restored."

Sarah glanced over to the window across the room, thinking of all the horrors and violent acts she had witnessed and been a part of.

"Yeah. The lowest of humanity has certainly crawled out of the gutters. I've had my fair share of run-ins with them." She peered down to her Glock, thinking of the angry, homely man she was forced shoot. That incident haunted her thoughts, and probably would for the rest of her life. It also reaffirmed why she no longer would cower under the thumb of criminals. "I've had to do things I thought I'd never have to do. At the end of the day, though, one must do what is necessary to protect oneself, and others."

Rick grabbed the brass doorknob of the apartment door, then looked upon Sarah's stern and focused face. "I agree. People shouldn't have to live in fear of being preyed on. I think if more people had that same mentality, this world wouldn't be filled with so many senseless acts of violence."

Powerless World

Sarah agreed with a tilt of her head. Before the home invasion, she didn't give much thought to owning a gun. She would've protected her family as she could, but resorting to taking a person's life never factored into the equation.

He opened the door. The boisterous arguing flooded into his dwelling. "What's going down right now around the city with all of the rioting and looting is just par for the course. There are so many people out of work because the economy is trash. The price of food has soared where most struggle to feed their families a decent meal. Tensions have been high for a while now. To me, that's why things escalated so fast. You combine all of the frustration and desperation with the power grid crashing like it did and you have the perfect storm."

That was one fact Sarah understood and had come to grips with. It was the name of the game, now. One that she was forced to play.

Rick leaned into the blinding darkness of the hallway. The light washed over the banister before his apartment. He checked down either side of the long stretch of hallway for added measure.

"All right. Come on." The wood floor creaked under his weight as he stepped out into the hallway. Sarah flanked him as she pulled his door closed. He headed toward the staircase. The floor creaked with every step they took.

A door opened to an apartment near the landing. Lingering within the shadows of the pitch-black apartment stood the silhouette of figure.

"Who's out there skulking about in the darkness like some damn thief?" a woman groused through strained breath. Her voice was raspy and full of agitation.

Rick stopped, then turned toward the space. The light illuminated a wrinkled, boney hand that grabbed the edge of the door. An elderly woman stood at the ready with a baseball bat clutched in her other hand.

"It's just me, Mrs. Culver."

She squinted at Rick, then Sarah. Her thin lips pursed as she struggled to lift the bat in the air. "Lord. What are you doing out here lurking in the dark like that? I could've hurt you and your little girlfriend here."

Rick opened his mouth, but Sarah beat him to it. "I'm not his girlfriend. We just met, and he was kind enough to help me out."

Sarah glanced to Rick, who diverted his gaze in embarrassment.

Mrs. Culver lowered the bat which wasn't too far off the ground. "Well, you better watch out for this one. He's a charmer for sure."

Rick cleared his throat. "We're heading up to the roof of the building to see if we can get a better view of the city. Like I told you before, just stay in your apartment and keep the door locked. I'll be by later to check on you. If you need anything, pound the wall with your cane, and I'll come over."

Mrs. Culver looked at Rick, then over to Sarah. A sly smirk slit across her face as she winked at him. "You two kids enjoy yourself on the roof."

"Thanks. Goodnight, Mrs. Culver."

The aged woman drifted back into the blackness of her apartment as Rick shut the door. The click of the deadbolt engaging played from the space.

Rick rolled his eyes, then rubbed his hand over his face. Sarah didn't need the light to see how red and flustered he was. "I'm sorry about that. She isn't all there and forgets things easily. Plus, she enjoys speaking her mind and embarrassing me."

Sarah found it amusing. It was the first time that day she'd had a good chuckle. It felt good. "Don't worry about it. She's sweet."

"She's something, all right," Rick added.

They left Mrs. Culver's apartment and headed up the stairs. The strident light guided the way through the murk. Each step creaked a warning as they bounded for the next floor.

More arguing and conflict bombarded Sarah. It sounded as if the doors to the apartments were open from the shouting that came from within.

Doors slammed.

The dense thumping of fists hammering the walls and doors echoed through the building. Accusations and threats of inadequacy were tossed around freely by the bickering and hostile dwellers inside.

Rick didn't stop or turn his head. He focused on the next flight of stairs down at the end of the corridor.

Another door slung open. A large, burly man stormed out in a huff as a nagging and spiteful female voice spewed crude and demeaning jargon at the brute.

His fingers were balled into fists as he stormed past. Sweat stains covered the front of his soiled white shirt that had a twinge of yellow to it. He mumbled something to himself.

"Awesome neighbors you have here," Sarah said.

Rick hit the landing to the next flight without missing a beat. "Like I said earlier, most of the people I know here are decent. Most."

The second flight of stairs was traversed with little effort. They swung around the banister, past the sealed doors that had little to no noise coming from them.

The remaining two floors were free of any hostile encounters. It was dead silent, considering how a portion of the people in the building were carrying on.

Rick stomped his way up the staircase to the dark-gray door that led out onto the roof. The barrage of fighting and discourse from the lower floors had all been squashed.

Silence filled the space between the two of them as he grabbed the door. Rick twisted the knob and pushed. The door swung open.

A gust of wind rushed into the narrow space. It smelled of smoke. Having the cool air brush over Sarah's skin was refreshing, even if it was tainted.

Sirens trumpeted through the dismal night skies. The noise seemed to have multiplied from what it was earlier with no end in sight.

Rick moved from the open door, allowing Sarah to step out. She moved out of his way as he closed the door.

He walked across the roof of the building to the far ledge. Sarah flanked him as her head turned from side to side, taking in the orange glow that lit up the horizon of the city.

Being on top of the roof and looking out over the blinding darkness that wasn't consumed by fires, made her feel as though the world wasn't burning down around her.

"Man, that is one hell of a bad view," Rick muttered in disbelief.

Off in the distance, Sarah spotted multiple lights tracing across the smoke-filled sky. The bleating of the chopper's rotors was faint, but easily heard without the restriction of the building dulling the noise.

"A woman told me that a few airliners collided somehow and crashed over the city." She pointed out the numerous blazes that canvased the dark and bleak landscape. "Looks like there's more fires going as well."

Rick set the flashlight on the ledge, then ran his fingers through his thick, black, wiry hair. "Yeah. I didn't see it, but I heard the explosion after they crashed. Sounded like a couple of damn bombs going off. I also heard that some of the transformers sparked and blew, causing fires in some of the older buildings around the city. Boston has its share of those. You mix all of that together with the civil unrest among the population and this is what you get."

"That's what I thought it was at first," Sarah said. "I was riding the subway when the power went out, so I ended up trapped down there. The ground shook overhead. I thought the world had ended or something."

Flashes of red and blue from police lights shone down the street. Sarah caught a brief glimpse before they vanished within the darkness.

Rick looked to Sarah. "You got any family out there in that mess?"

"Yeah. My best friend and husband." Sarah dipped her chin, then peered off into the fiery distance of the burning city. "I was supposed to meet my friend at Copley Place earlier today, but that never happened."

"And your husband?" Rick countered without missing a beat.

"I'm not sure where he is, to be honest. He left to go on a weekend trip with his friend. I haven't heard from him since early this morning. No cell service."

"Well, I imagine the both of them are all right. Nothing to worry about," Rick reassured as best he could.

Sarah bowed her head, acknowledging the kind words. It was hard to accept, considering the state of things. She didn't know how widespread the blackout was or if it was just contained to Boston. For all she knew, it could've been global since they were cut off from the rest of the world. That thought scared her.

"They probably are. I would just like to know to be sure." Sarah glanced to the Glock, then stuffed it into the waistband of her trousers. She felt safe for the moment, at least safe enough not to need it in her hand. If things went south, retrieving the weapon wouldn't be an issue. "I was heading to my friend's place when I was forced off the street and to this building. I need to find her and make sure she's all right. We're practically sisters and all."

Rick leaned forward and pressed the palm of his hands to the edge of the roof. He craned his neck and peered to the street below. "If it's all the same, you might wait until morning before leaving. Best to keep off the streets for the time being. It's not safe for anyone down there right now."

That was Sarah's plan. Striking out into the city now was not going to benefit anyone. It would only serve those who sought out the weak and looked to take advantage of any people unlucky enough to cross their paths.

Come daybreak, Sarah would get back on the move and head to Mandy's place. Hopefully, by then, the authorities would have regained control, and the city would be back under the rule of law.

"I didn't think anyone else came up here except for me," a soft feminine voice called out from the darkness.

Sarah flinched, then spun on her heels with her hand reaching for the Glock.

A flicker of light lit up the woman's face as she ignited the end of a cigarette.

Rick grabbed Sarah's wrist, thwarting her notion to draw the weapon. "Whoa. Hold on, there."

Powerless World

Sarah panted from the sudden appearance of the woman who lingered in the shadows off to the side of the entrance to the roof. Her heart hammered as she exhaled. "Do you know her?"

"Christ, lady," the woman exclaimed in fright. "On edge, much?"

"Yeah. I know her," Rick confirmed. "She lives a floor above me. Diane, why are you up here hiding in the dark?"

The woman took a drag from the cigarette. The end burned an orangish-red. "You know, had to get some distance away from Brad. Things were getting heated between us earlier, and I needed some air. Taking a stroll out on the street didn't seem wise with everything going on. So here I am."

Rick sighed. "I thought you two had worked things out and everything was better."

Diane shrugged. Smoke blew from her lips. She wiped her hands across her face. "They were for a bit, but, no offense, Rick, he's a man, and doesn't get it at times. I love the big, dumb ape, but just get tired of the things he does at times."

Sarah heard sniffles linger from the distraught woman. Although cast in shadows, Sarah caught a glimpse of Diane's face. She figured she was maybe in her late to early twenties from the sound of her voice.

Rick looked to Sarah with a lost look on his face. "No offense taken. Did you, um, want to talk about it?"

Diane scoffed. "I appreciate the offer, Rick, but I don't think you'd understand. As Brad said, it's a woman thing. I'll be fine. Just need to cool off and all. Besides, you've got your girlfriend with you. I don't want to be a bother"

"Why does everyone think I'm your girlfriend," Sarah muttered to him.

Rick shrugged, then threw up his hands. "I really don't know."

Sarah rolled her eyes, then shook her head. "Yeah. Right."

Diane puffed on the cigarette while staring off at the dismal night sky.

Sarah felt for the young woman, and could relate to how she was feeling. Russell had similar shortcomings which made Sarah mad at times, but they always worked it out.

Being in a relationship was never easy, and at times, the struggle to even be around them was hard as hell. At the end of the day, though, if someone love a person, then nothing was impossible to work out.

Sarah was realizing that fact even more.

CHAPTER TWENTY-TWO

RUSSELL

Thomas sat in his rocking chair, angry from listening to Cathy retell the day's events that had led them to his doorstep in the middle of the night.

A mixture of emotions twisted the old man's face from shock to a scowl. His wrinkled brow furrowed. Heavy breaths blew through his nostrils like a raging bull. His gaunt, boney fingers rapped against the scuffed wooden arm of his chair.

"I can't believe Mr. Wright would stoop to such tactics. I always knew that man was garbage, but didn't think it was possible for him to sink any lower," Thomas vented.

Cathy nodded in agreement from the plush leather chair she was resting on. A towel dangled from the arm of the chair. She pulled the light-brown blanket, draped over her shoulders, a hair tighter. "Yeah. Me too. He's had his goons snooping around my place for some time. Doing little things here and there to try and make me sell or just abandon the property. It didn't escalate until recently, though."

Anger surged over Thomas's face, and his fingers balled into fists. "I have half a mind to head over to that bastard's place right now with the double barrel and serve up some old school justice."

Russell thought he'd lose that fight without much effort from the opposition. It was a death sentence for the old man who struggled to even walk.

"Just settle down over there. Your blood pressure is going to go through the roof. You know how it gets when you get excited like this." Cathy motioned with her hands for Thomas to relax and take it easy, but the gruff and hardened man wasn't looking to let Marcus slide on what he'd done.

He took a deep breath in through his nose, then exhaled the frustration through his thin lips. Butch lifted his head from the rug to check on his handler.

"Yeah, yeah. I know. Just chaps my ass is all. You and Max are like family. Either of you could've been seriously hurt or killed for Christ's sake." He glanced to Russell who rested on the couch in front of the fireplace. A wadded-up, sodden towel sat in his lap. His clothes were still damp, but drying from the heat given off by the fire. "I'm glad Mr. Cage was there to help out, despite how he arrived and all."

"We are too," Cathy added.

"You're lucky to be alive, son. Sorry about your friend. I can't imagine how harrowing that must have been for you."

Russell offered a gracious tilt of his head. "Thanks. I was fortunate that Cathy and Max found me when they did. I was hurt and contending with a mountain lion."

Powerless World

"The wilderness can be a beautiful place, but dangerous if you're not careful," Thomas said.

Butch laid his head back on the rug near Max's. Both animals rested on the floor without so much as a squabble between the two beasts. Max laid motionless, dead to the world with only a twitch of his ears to let the others know he was still awake.

Thomas rubbed his chin as he mumbled to himself. "The sheriff needs to get involved and arrest that dirtbag. I would say let's call him up now, but the damn phones don't work. Haven't for some time. Same for the power. Cut off without any warning earlier, and it hasn't even tried to come back on yet."

The modified lanterns were still lit and provided enough light in the cabin to get the general lay of the land. It was up in the air as to how long they'd last, though.

Cathy stood from the chair and grabbed a log next to the fireplace. She fed the beefy bark to the dwindling fire. "I'll worry about speaking with the sheriff at some point."

She prodded the scorched wood with the poker as Thomas gave her a peculiar stare. From what Russell could tell, he didn't care for her response. "At some point? This needs to be handled fast. The longer you wait, the less likely that piece of crap will pay for what he did."

The fire roared back to life. Crackles escaped the charred blocks of wood.

Cathy placed the poker back on the stand and sat back down. "I'm more concerned with Amber at the moment. I haven't been able to reach her since the power went out. Who knows what kind of damage that solar storm did or how wide spread it is? I've got insurance on the place that will take care of most of everything that went up in the fire. Plus, I've already filed a report, and you see what good that did. A part of me thinks the sheriff is in Marcus's back pocket. Wouldn't surprise me if he was. Marcus has the town under his thumb."

"I imagine Amber is fine. She's just as stubborn and hardheaded as you. Don't know of anyone who would want to take on that young lady."

Cathy rubbed her hand over her face while glancing at Russell. Bickering with the old man didn't seem to be what she had in mind when she decided to trek through the wilderness and rain at night.

Thomas glanced at Russell again, then back over to Cathy. His tense body relaxed and his balled fists unclenched. It looked as though he knew he was digging under her skin, and he needed to tone it down. "I didn't know you had already spoken with the sheriff about all of the troubles you were having with Marcus. I can't believe the corruption in this place. I left the city to get away from that, and here we are right smack dab in the thick of it again."

Cathy sighed, then lowered her arm to her thighs. "Listen, Thomas. I know you're just concerned and all, but I will handle everything as I see fit. I didn't come by here to get lectured until the early hours of morning. So, if we could just drop it for now, that would be great."

Silence fell over the room. Tension clung to the air like a bad stench. The crackling of the fireplace and wind howling filled the space between them as Cathy leaned back in her chair.

Russell rubbed his hands up and down his thighs, then cut his gaze over to Thomas who rocked in his chair. The ends of his skeletal fingers tapped his gray, stubbled chin as he stared at the flames. Russell didn't do well with tension, especially when it was between others, and he was in the middle of the squabble.

"Could I trouble you for a drink of water?" he asked.

Thomas's gaze lingered on the fire.

Cathy sighed, then slung the blanket from her shoulders. "Come here. I'll show you where the kitchen is."

She stood up while looking at Thomas. Russell had seen that agitated expression many times before on Sarah's face.

Max stirred. A sharp ruff emitted from his snout as he rolled over to his stomach. He yawned, then stretched his front legs. The ends of his claws snagged on the material of the rug as he gave his coat a good shake.

Cathy skirted the arm of the chair and grabbed the lantern that was on top of the round table. Russell dropped the towel to the floor and followed her through the dimly lit house with Max flanking them both.

Butch watched the trio. His ears flicked from their footfalls over the wood planks, but he didn't leave his handler's side.

"I love that old man to death, but lord, he grates on my nerves at times," Cathy groused.

"He reminds me of my grandparents—coarse and rough around the edges," Russell responded through a whisper. "Listening to him speak made me think of those old movies done back in the day. One thing is certain, he cares about you."

Cathy lifted the lantern up as she hugged the corner of the wall. "He does and I know he's only being protective, but it's overbearing at times. It doesn't get on my nerves normally, but with everything going down as it is, I'm in no mood for a lecture. He should know that."

Russell paused, then peered back to the living room as Cathy continued into the long, narrow kitchen. Max brushed past him in pursuit of his master.

Thomas was still seated in his rocking chair, looking off into space. The wrinkles around his mouth sagged as he sniffled. Below that hardened exterior and gruff demeanor a soft center oozed out.

Butch had gotten off the floor and stood at his side as Thomas ran his fingers over the crown of his head. The dog looked in Russell's direction with a fixed, stern gaze.

"Cups are in here," Cathy informed with a cheerless tone while pointing at one of the upper cabinets. "You can get some water from the tap."

"Thanks."

Cathy set the lantern on the marble white countertop. "I'll leave this here for you. I'm going to take Max to the laundry room, and get him some chow. If you want to catch a few winks of sleep, Thomas has a few extra bedrooms. I'm probably going to lay down and rest before we head out. Bathroom is down the hall there along with the bedrooms. First door on the right."

"Got it. I–"

"Come on, boy." Cathy patted her leg once, then walked past Russell. Max followed close behind. Both vanished in the murk of the hallway, leaving Russell alone in the kitchen.

Being stuck in the middle of a bickering match wasn't Russell's ideal plan. If he had his druthers, they'd find some way of getting on the road and moving on.

He opened the cabinet. The hinges squeaked from lack of oil on their joints. Light from the lantern illuminated the interior of the cabinet. On the bottom shelf, a bottle of Knob Creek caught Russell's attention.

His mouth watered. His tongue slid across his lips from the thought of taking the spirit. Excitement swelled inside him like a kid who found an unwrapped gift at Christmas.

One taste. That's all. Just something to take the edge off.

It was never just a single taste or sip. One always turned into two, and before he knew it, half the bottle was gone.

Russell wrestled with indecision. A bounty of pros and cons played inside his head. It had been some time since he had taken the painkillers, and he figured he'd be all right to at least have that sip.

"Well, are you going to grab the bottle or not?" an angry voice inquired.

"Umm, what?" Russell turned around to face the old man who sounded more agitated than he was before. "I was getting a cup for that drink of water."

He reached inside the cupboard and grabbed a glass from the bottom shelf.

Thomas stood at the opening of the kitchen with Butch at his side. A disgruntled expression covered his face as he eyed Russell.

"Sure, you were." He crossed his arms. "I know the look a man gets when he hasn't had a taste for some time. Hell, I've been there."

Russell sat the glass on the counter, then looked at Thomas. "It has been a shitty couple of days. Just looking to take the edge off."

"Hell, son. Given that you were in a plane crash and dealing with that mess at her place, you probably need one. I know I do." Thomas pointed at the cabinet. "Grab me a glass and the Knob Creek, will ya?"

He didn't have to ask twice.

Russell jumped at the chance. He flung open the door to the cabinet, grabbed another glass, and the bottle of liquor.

A flickering light from down the hall where Cathy was shone on the floor near the kitchen. Thomas leaned away from the wall and craned his neck. He motioned with his hand for Russell to hurry up.

"What's wrong?" Russell inquired.

"Cathy doesn't like when I drink. Says it won't mix well with the blood pressure medication I'm taking. She's already pissed.

179

I don't want to piss her off anymore. Believe me, you don't want to see that."

Russell didn't doubt it. Cathy was a strong, independent woman, and didn't take crap from anybody. It reminded him of Sarah. Both were forces to be reckoned with when they were upset.

He handed Thomas the bottle, and scooped up the lantern and both glasses.

The two men and Butch skulked through the cabin to the entryway. Thomas grabbed his coat from the hook and tossed it to Russell.

Going outside while being damp wasn't what Russell had in mind, but if it meant getting a drink and satisfying his craving, then it would be well worth it.

Thomas slipped on another coat, then cracked open the door. Butch squeezed his way through the narrow opening as Thomas nodded to Russell.

Like thieves in the night, they left the house without a single sound.

Thomas walked across the porch and sat the bottle on the railing. His hand burrowed into his coat pocket as he looked out over the dense cluster of trees that were swallowed by the night.

The rain had all but stopped. Nothing more than a trickle fell and pinged off the covering. A brisk breeze bit at Russell's hands and face, making him shiver.

"How long have you lived up here?" Russell set the glass on the railing near the bottle as he skimmed over the blinding darkness.

Owls hooted from the woods.

The shuffling of leaves nearby peaked Butch's curiosity. His ears twitched, then stood on end as he searched for the source.

Thomas pulled his hand out of his coat pocket. A crushed package of cigarettes was clutched in his grasp. He opened the top and pulled one out. "Oh, hell. Long enough to not remember how long. Want one?"

He presented the package to Russell, who refused the offer with a subtle shake of his head. "No thanks. Another bad habit I'm trying to quit"

"Suit yourself." Thomas shrugged, then slipped the rich tobacco stick between his lips. "I've been working on this same pack for months. Only smoke when I'm stressed and all. Helps calm the nerves."

Russell could relate. Everyone had their vices and dealt with things in their own way. For some, it was smoking. For others, like him, it was drinking.

Thomas crammed the package back into his coat pocket. He lit the tip and puffed on the butt. He glanced over his shoulder at the cabin as smoke blew from his mouth. "Are you going to crack open that bottle, or are we just going to stand here all-night thinking about it?"

Cathy wasn't the only one who was in a foul mood, that much was certain. Russell kept his mouth shut to avoid saying something he might regret.

He pulled the top free of the bottle and poured the whiskey.

Thomas grabbed one of glasses. He removed the cigarette from his mouth and gulped down the stout spirit in one fell swoop. "Man, that's some good stuff."

Russell followed suit and knocked back the shot of whiskey in his glass. The full-bodied spirit was sweet and had a woody taste that lingered on his tongue. He relished in the moment as the liquor coursed through his body.

"That's rather smooth." Russell licked his lips dry.

Thomas tilted his head. "Yeah. The store in town doesn't have a deep selection of hard liquor. It's pretty limited up here. One makes do with what they have."

Russell doled out another shot in his glass. He offered another round to the old man. "Are you a prepper like Cathy?"

Thomas held up a hand, refusing the drink. "Living up here, you sort of have to be. There aren't many resources close by, so you have to learn to be self-reliant and handle matters on your own. Neighbors are few and far between. Cathy is the closest person to me for miles." Thomas took another drag from the cigarette. He peered back over his shoulder again as if he was on the lookout for her. "Do you ever stick your foot in your mouth? I seem to have a knack for doing that these days. Could be old age, or because I'm just a crotchety bastard. That's what I've been told, anyway."

"All the time, or so my wife would say. Well, soon to be ex-wife maybe. I don't know," Russell answered without missing a beat. "Over the past year, it feels like the heel of my shoe has been glued to my mouth all of the time. I'm either saying the wrong thing, or not saying enough. It's almost like I'm damned if I do and damned if I don't." Russell threw his head back. The shot vanished in a blink.

Thomas blew the smoke from his mouth, then squashed the end on the railing. He flicked the crumpled bud to the ground.

Butch yawned, revealing his fangs that glistened from the solar light reflecting off the canines. "Well, that seems to be what we're good for, I'd imagine. I know I drove my late wife crazy. When it comes to those I love and care for, I get overzealous, speak before I have a chance to process the words that dump out of my mouth." Thomas lowered his head, then reached down to his knees. He grumbled under his breath as he massaged his knee caps. "Damn body isn't what it used to be. It's falling apart day by day."

Powerless World

Russell could relate about speaking before thinking. He had done that more times than he could count. "I think at the end of the day, we do our best and try to learn from our mistakes. We're never perfect, and we won't be. As long as we try to do better than we did the day before, I consider that a win."

Thomas lifted his leg, then stretched it out. A wide yawn overtook him, and he covered his mouth. "And on that note, I think I'm going to retire. It's way past my bedtime." He turned toward the cabin, and nodded. "I've got an extra room in there if you want to get some shuteye."

"Thanks. I'll head in here shortly," Russell said with a somber tone.

Defeat weighed on his shoulders. He glanced at the shot glass, then sighed from the guilt that swarmed him. Sarah was there for him at all times, but he drew away from her and ran to the arms of liquor instead. Perhaps it was the fact that he felt like a failure in protecting his family. Afterall, that's what a man did, right? He wanted her back more than life itself, but he hadn't shown her that. Words only did so much, but actions spoke volumes.

Thomas stared at Russell, then placed his wrinkled hand on his shoulder. "You know, son, we all make mistakes. Some are worse than others, but at the end of the day, it's never too late to make things right. I don't know your situation, and don't really need to, but if you love this woman with all of your heart, you need not only tell her, but show her as well. Whatever you're battling, you can overcome it. Just dig deep and fight back."

Poignant words that struck to the heart of the matter. It was something that Russell needed to be reminded of, a swift kick in the ass to keep him focused on getting Sarah back, if it wasn't too late.

He offered Thomas a warm smile followed by a grateful nod. "Thanks. I appreciate it."

"Not a problem. Like I said, I've had experience in such matters. Just passing on the wisdom."

Thomas winked, then limped toward the front door with Butch by his side. Subtle grunts lingered from his lips as he paused. He peered over his shoulder, and said, "Thanks for entertaining this old fool for a spell. It was nice to have a drink and converse with someone."

"Likewise," Russell said.

Thomas opened the door and disappeared inside the dark dwelling.

Russell tilted the opening of the bottle over his glass without thinking about it. He stared at the base of the empty shot glass. His body craved the liquor, but he didn't want to pour the shot.

His gaze flitted to the now cloudless sky filled with stars. He set the bottle further down the railing to avoid the temptation.

Both hands grabbed hold of the wood. The sharp ends of the plank poked his sensitive palms, but Russell didn't care. He breathed in deep, then exhaled through pursed lips.

A barrage of thoughts flashed through his head. Everything from Sarah to the plane crash coalesced in his mind. In that moment, Russell decided things were going to change. Whatever he had to do, would be done. No mountain would be too big for him to scale or river too deep cross. Making things right with Sarah and getting her back was all he wanted. Anything else wouldn't do.

What tomorrow held for him was up in the air. It was a new day that would no doubt present a slew of challenges, both mentally and physically.

Russell would have to overcome his demons and fight like hell, but he was ready for the coming battle.

Powerless World

CHAPTER TWENTY-THREE

SARAH

Dreams were what nightmares, and monsters, were made of. An endless affliction of unrest plagued Sarah for what fraction of sleep she had gotten. Most of the night consisted of her speaking with Diane on the roof, then tossing and turning on Rick's couch. Diane had been grateful for Sarah taking the time to speak with her, which somewhat countered the awful sleep Sarah got.

The rigid cushions knotted her back, and the uneasiness of sleeping in a stranger's apartment lingered in her thoughts, keeping her on edge. Rick hadn't tried anything, or come across as anything less than a gentleman, but still, she was cautious.

The biggest culprit of stealing her rest was not only Russell's state of well-being, but the tormentor of her dreams. The Creeper.

Powerless World

Sarah woke in a dazed fright, terrified by the evil man who sought her out even when she slept. The Creeper never left her thoughts. He was nestled in the black matter of her brain, waiting for his moment to strike.

A wave of panic washed over Sarah as she sat up from the couch. Strident rays from the sun shone through the bay windows across the apartment and hit her face. She squinted and diverted her gaze. Her hand shielded the light as her eyes adjusted.

Something didn't feel right.

Her fingers closed as if by muscle memory around the grip of her gun that wasn't there. The Glock was gone. Missing. What happened to her weapon?

Sarah tossed her legs from the couch to the floor. The soles of her shoes hit something firm and dense. She lifted her foot.

The Glock was on the rug. Did she drop it in the middle of the night, or did something else happen? She peered over the back of the couch for Rick, but he wasn't anywhere in sight.

She heard movement from the room past the kitchen. Footfalls creaked over the wooden planks of the floor. Rick walked past the cracked open door while putting on a shirt.

Sarah grumbled from being tired, then turned around. She retrieved the Glock from the floor, and set it in her lap. Her body deflated against the back of the couch. Lack of sleep was a bitch.

The palms of her hands rubbed up and down her face. She didn't need a mirror to see what a mess she had to be. The sleepiness that lingered told the tale.

Sarah grabbed the Glock from her lap and leaned forward. She pushed up off the couch. The muscles in her back were stiff and stole her breath when she straightened out.

She secured the Glock in the waistband of her trousers, then stretched. A yawn fled her open mouth as Rick flanked her.

"How did you sleep?" he inquired.

Sarah flinched, then pulled her arms in. "All right, I suppose." She didn't want to be rude. Afterall, he had opened his home to her.

He patted the top of the couch with his hand. "I know it's not the most comfortable thing in the world to sleep on. You could've taken the bed, and I would've slept out here. I wouldn't have minded."

Sarah gave a warm smile. This wasn't her place, and she didn't feel right kicking him out of his bedroom. Besides, sleeping in another man's bed made her feel uneasy, all things considered. "The couch worked. Your hospitality is appreciated. Thank you for everything."

Rick nodded. "It was my pleasure. I wouldn't have felt right leaving you out there in that mess."

"I should probably get on my way and check on my friend to make sure she's ok." Sarah dipped her chin and scanned for her purse. She was burning daylight, even though it was early in the morning.

"I believe you set it on the floor near the entryway," Rick pointed out.

She turned toward the far wall. Her purse was on the floor, leaning against the front leg of the tall table. "Thanks."

Sarah walked across the room, stiff as a board. She bent over and wrangled the straps. Her head throbbed from the movement, and she hurt all over. The twisted knots in her back and neck ravaged her body. She mumbled, then sighed as she stood up while rubbing her temples.

Aspirin. That's what she needed to combat the dull, nagging pain. She cracked open her purse and sifted through the contents. Her fingers pushed the makeup and other personal items out of the way. A bottle of generic pain reliever caught her eye.

"Is the water running, by chance?" Perhaps it was a silly question, but Sarah wasn't sure if it would be running or not. "I've got a headache and need something to wash it down. I wasn't sure since it looks like the power is still out."

The digital clock on the black stove and microwave were blank, void of any green tinted numbers on the face of the appliances.

"Um, it should be for now, I think. Let me check." Rick turned on his heels and made for the kitchen. He grabbed the handle to the faucet and lifted it up. Water sputtered from the spout.

"For now, looks like it." He grabbed a small plastic cup from the strainer next to him and filled it up.

Sarah pressed down on the top of the bottle and twisted. The cap popped and spun lose. She tilted the bottle at an angle, then gave it a single shake.

The brown coated pills jostled about inside the container. It wasn't full, but she only needed two for now.

"Here you go." Rick extended the plastic cup to Sarah.

She dumped out two of the pills into her palm, then tossed them into her mouth. The water chased the pain reliever down her throat. She hoped it would kick in fast. Sarah gulped the remainder of the tepid water, then licked her lips.

"Thanks." She handed the cup back to Rick.

He set it on the table next to the door as Sarah slipped the straps of her purse over her shoulder.

"You're welcome." Rick stood in the entryway, looking at Sarah. His brow lifted as indecision swirled in his eyes. The palms of his hands rubbed up and down the fronts of his stressed denim jeans as he lowered his head.

"Something on your mind?" Sarah probed. It wasn't difficult to read that he wanted to ask her something.

"Yeah. I know you can take care of yourself and all—" He glanced to the Glock she had secured in the waistband of her trousers. "—but I'd feel better if you'd allow me to escort you to your friend's place. With all the craziness going on out there, it wouldn't be right for me not to at least offer up some help."

Sarah peered out of the bay windows to the sun that had chased the darkness away. She wasn't as worried about trekking through the city now that night was done. It seemed less intimidating than when the darkness had blanketed the powerless streets.

Besides, she didn't want to be an inconvenience to Rick any more than she already had been. Sarah hated feeling like a bother, and fought most times to do things on her own to avoid putting others out.

"I appreciate the offer, but I think I'll be fine. Hopefully, the police have gotten all the riffraff off the streets. You've already done so much, I couldn't possibly take up any more of your time."

Rick dismissed Sarah's assumption with a flick of his wrist, then shook his head. "It wouldn't be taking up anymore of my time. It's not like I'm going to watch TV or anything like that. The power is still out. You would be giving me something to do. Take my mind off this crappy, cramped apartment and my current employment situation."

Sarah thought on it some more, and figured it wouldn't hurt. Having him with her might keep any unsavory types from trying to rob her or anything worse. "Yeah. Why not."

"Great." A warm smile broke across Rick's stubble-ridden face. He clapped his hands together, and drifted back into the kitchen. "Give me five minutes, and I'll be good to go." Rick rushed through the kitchen toward his room. He hugged the jamb and vanished from her sight.

Powerless World

Sarah patted her back pocket for her phone. The slim device was nestled within the trousers. Her fingers gripped the top and pulled it out as she waited for Rick.

She figured the battery was dead since it hadn't been charged in over a day. The phone hadn't been keeping a charge well. It was on her to-do list to get it replaced.

The screen flashed and acted as though it was going to load, but died instead. She thumbed the power button again. The phone refused to cycle on.

Great.

Rick came out of his bedroom just as Sarah placed the dead device back into her pocket. He secured his Glock behind his back in the waistband of his jeans. The bottom of the shirt was pulled over the firearm to conceal its presence.

"Still no signal?" he inquired. "I haven't even bothered with mine since early yesterday."

"Don't know. Phone won't turn on," Sarah groaned. "I think the battery has died or something. You wouldn't happen to have a portable charger or anything like that, would you?"

Rick glanced over his apartment, deep in thought as he scrunched his lips. "Not that I can think of off the top of my head, but I still have moving boxes I haven't gone through yet. Could be one in there."

"Don't worry about it. I'll deal with it later. There probably isn't a signal anyway," Sarah retorted. Rick bowed his head and adjusted his shirt as she starred at him. "You sure you want to come? I'm more than capable of handling it on my own."

"I have no doubts that you can," Rick countered with a wry grin. "Just consider me an insurance policy incase things get dicey."

"Insurance policy, huh," Sarah parroted. "Are you expecting trouble?"

"Given the state of things out there right now, yeah. I plan for the worst, and hope for the best. When the shit hits the fan, people become unpredictable and lose their minds. If and when the authorities get a handle on things, then I'll think otherwise. Until then, you have to keep your guard up and be vigilant. There's always some snake in the grass ready to strike." Rick opened the door to his apartment, and offered a wink before peering out into the silent hallway.

The boisterous ruckus from the night before had all but died. No heavy footfalls hammered the floors. The shouting had waned to a dull silence. Either the residents were dead in their apartments, or they were sound asleep.

Rick ventured out into the hallway with Sarah flanking him. She pulled the door to and checked the knob, making sure it was secured and locked.

She followed him down the hallway to the staircase. He didn't appear to be as worried as he was last night. The dark had a way of pushing people to the edge of their own fears, regardless if there was a threat looming or not.

They traversed the staircase down to the first floor, which was void of any people milling about. Only the sounds of their shoes filled the hallway.

The main entrance to the building was still shut, but the window had been busted out. Shards of broken glass carpeted the tile floor. Each piece crunched under their feet as they approached.

Rick peered at the few apartments that lined both sides of the corridor. The doors were shut with no evidence of a break in or foul play.

He stopped, then glanced past the stairs to the remaining apartments that went farther back into the building. The natural light from the sun shining in through the window struggled to make it to the deep recesses of the structure. A blanket of darkness hung over the hallway, making it difficult to see.

"Do you think anyone broke in over the night?" Sarah inquired.

Rick craned his neck and squinted, then shook his head. "I don't think so. Looks like they just busted out the window and didn't bother coming in. I imagine there's a lot of young people out trashing stuff just because they can."

That wouldn't surprise Sarah. Delinquents seemed to be drawn to chaos and upheaval like a moth to a flame. Any chance they got to cause havoc, they were ready and willing to jump in.

She had seen it enough times before this catastrophe that had shut the entire city down. Subway stations were the worst and other less than desirable places within Boston were breeding grounds for the unruly youth.

The crunch of glass under their feet echoed down the hallway. Sarah flanked Rick and mimicked his movement.

He peered through the missing window to the street. He grabbed the handle and pulled the stout door away from the jamb. He leaned against the wall lined with mailboxes and surveyed the area. It only took a few seconds of him craning his neck before he waved his hand.

"Looks clear. Come on." Rick advanced out onto the concrete landing with Sarah close behind. They looked over the street in both directions. It was void of any activity.

The sky had a gray tint, which made it murky and dull. Brief pockets within the clouds allowed the sun to shine through. Smoke tainted the air. The buildings around them hadn't suffered any sort of structural damage from the fires that had sprung up all across the city. Given how many fires burned across the city, she was glad to see buildings free of damage.

"What do you think?" Sarah probed as they moved down the stairs to the sidewalk. "Do you think the police have gotten the city under control?"

Rick's head was on a swivel, looking down the streets for any activity that could be cause for concern. His face was stern and focused, fixed on the task at hand. Everything seemed to be all right, but he didn't look convinced.

He shrugged. "I don't know if they have or not. Hard to tell. It's still early in the morning. I imagine most everyone kept off the streets just to be safe. The cops are probably handling areas that need it most. There's no way they could cover the entire city without additional support."

Sarah followed his gaze. Most of the cars she remembered seeing around the area were still there. A portion of the vehicles had suffered damage. Busted windows and dents peppered the steel bodies. No doubt from vandals.

"Do you think the coast guard or military will be sent in to help out?"

"I'd think eventually they would, but it hinges on how widespread this blackout is and if the police aren't able to get things back under control. If it's just Boston, then maybe. If it covers more cities or states even, then that's a different ballgame all together. They'll have to send in the military to keep the peace, or at least, get everything under control."

Rick looked at Sarah who was scanning over the abandoned cars and nearby buildings. "How far away is your friend's place?"

Sarah pointed to the east. "She's on the other side of town. It's not that far if you take a car or public transportation, but on foot, it'll take a lot longer."

That was the last thing Sarah wanted to do, but she didn't see any other choice. The subways had all stopped. Buses and taxis were an unknown, but she doubted they'd be running due to the state of things within the city. As far as she could tell, they were screwed.

Rick turned on his heels, then glanced down the sidewalk. "Come on. I might have a way for us to get there."

CHAPTER TWENTY-FOUR

RUSSELL

A ball of nerves and tension laid claim to Russell's body. What else was new? It was a feeling Russell had become all too familiar with.

The Knob Creek that sloshed about in his gut relaxed him some, but not enough to help him sleep. For the better part of the night, Russell paced the narrow opening between the twin-size bed and the other junk Thomas had crammed into the tiny bedroom.

He contemplated finishing off the remainder of the spirit. There wasn't much left in the brown-tinted bottle. Not for Russell, anyway. A few topped off glasses and it would be gone. Simple as that. But that wasn't the issue.

If he did drink it, his mind wouldn't be as sharp, and he couldn't risk that. Threats loomed large all around, and he didn't know when they would spring their heads. A constant battle waged within his body. To drink or not. He was unsure if he could hold off the feeling.

In the back of his mind, Russell could see Sarah's disappointed expression for not being strong enough to hold off the temptation. She'd have her brow furrowed and arms folded across her chest as she tapped her foot. That was the worst part of drinking. The hangover paled in comparison to the sadness that washed over her face. He was tired of being responsible for such an expression. Things had to change.

Russell roamed about the cabin in the dark until morning broke and the others got up. He tried his hand at grabbing some sleep on the couch in front of the fireplace, but it wasn't in the cards. As soon as he closed his eyes, a million thoughts pelted his brain.

Both Max and Butch scrambled down the hallway. Their claws fought for traction on the wooden floor. Heavy pants filled the silence of the log house as the animals navigated the furniture.

Russell slouched on the couch with his head resting on the cushions. His body dripped with exhaustion, even though his mind was wound tight as a rope.

A cup of dark coffee, black with nothing extra, was what he craved. Perhaps if he threw in a red bull for good measure he might be a functional human being. The liquid breakfast of champions.

"Max. Where are you?" Cathy belted from the other end of the cabin. "I don't want you rummaging about Thomas's place."

The large dogs skirted the tables and chairs in haste, and found their way to Russell. He reeled back as they closed in on either side of him.

Max wasn't so much on his list of animals to be afraid of. Although big, he wasn't unpleasant. Butch, on the other hand, knocked him to the ground and almost used his face as a chew toy.

"They're in here," Russell called out.

His voice was unsteady, filled with trepidation as Butch stared at him from the front of the couch. The clipped ears of the cane corso were taut, and his body rigid. He didn't deviate his eyes from Russell which was unsettling and intimidating.

Max licked Russell's hand, then pawed at his forearm. A moan, then a sharp bark boomed from his snout as he tossed his head back.

Russell rubbed the crown of Max's head. The gentle German shepherd leaned into his touch. His tongue dangled out the side of his snout with joy.

"You like that, huh?" Russell said to Max as he panted.

Butch nudged his leg, but didn't offer as warm of a welcome.

Russell hesitated on petting the beast for fear that he might lose his hand, or worse.

"Max," Cathy called again, this time from the kitchen. His head tilted to the side, but he didn't budge. She peered into the living room, and said, "He isn't bothering you, is he?"

"Not at all," Russell responded with a shake of his head. "They're keeping me company. Well, Max is. I feel like a prisoner with the warden staring at me with Butch, though."

"He looks like that most times," Thomas chimed in with a raised voice from the hallway. "Did he nudge your leg?"

"Yeah," Russell answered.

"He needs to go outside to do his business. Can you take him out for me?" Thomas inquired.

Cathy shook her head as she walked toward Russell. "Here. I'll take them out."

Russell held up his hand, stopping her. "It's no problem. Some fresh air might do me some good and wake me up."

"You sure?" Cathy retorted with an elevated brow.

"Yeah. It's the least I can do. Besides, I'd like to stay on Max's good side and stay off Butch's shit list if at all possible."

Max dropped to the floor as Russell leaned forward. His tail wagged with excitement. He groaned, then turned toward the front door.

Butch bulldozed past Russell after Max, forcing Russell up against the couch. The dog was a brute and carried himself as such. His rigid posture and unfriendly disposition made that apparent. It could've been because he wasn't used to Russell, or perhaps he just didn't like him for whatever reason. Hard to tell. As long as he didn't try to claw his face again, it didn't matter.

"Hey," Cathy said to Russell as he moved around the couch after the dogs. "Butch is a cane corso. It took me a bit to figure out his breed."

"And?"

"Those dogs are inherently independent, loyal, and headstrong," Cathy said. "They have to have a firm owner to keep them in check. If one is not careful, they can easily take over the leadership role and become the dominant aggressive."

Russell glanced to the large beast, then back to Cathy. "So, you're saying that I just need to be more firm with him?"

"It wouldn't hurt." Cathy peered at Thomas who was in the kitchen, rummaging through his upper cabinets. "That's why Butch obeys and acts the way he does around him. Because the leadership has been defined and kept in place."

Both dogs groaned, then barked at the front door. Nature called and they were getting impatient.

Russell tilted his head. Max groaned again and barked as he approached the duo. "Yeah, yeah. I'm coming. Got to go that bad, huh?" He wormed his way through the dogs, nudging them in the sides to move them out of his way. More groans of anxiousness loomed from their snouts.

The door couldn't open fast enough as Butch took the lead and forced his way out through the narrow gap. Max flanked the hulking brute as the two dogs raced from the porch and out into the chilly morning.

Russell grabbed a coat from the hook near the side of the entryway, and put it on as he walked outside.

A cool, crisp breeze whipped about as he zipped the coat up just below his neck. Both hands burrowed into the warmth of the wool pockets as he walked toward the railing.

Watching the sun's rays filter through the trees that surrounded the property was serene and calming. Although he longed for the concrete jungle, he could appreciate the amazing scenery before him.

A heavy dew coated the grass in front of Thomas's cabin. Both Max and Butch split up and searched the grounds for the perfect place to relieve themselves.

The rustling of leaves from opposite sides of the property drew Russell's attention. Their tails stood erect while they sifted through the foliage.

"All right, guys. You about done?" he yelled.

The dogs rooted through the tall grass and dense verdure for a bit longer before they came running out. They dashed across the open plot of ground before the cabin and made a beeline for Russell.

Max stopped on a dime, then Butch. Their ears flicked as they skimmed over the nearby trees. Something had caught their attention.

It was probably just another animal or perhaps the wind moving the leaves and branches of the trees. After all, they were out in the wilderness. There were bound to be animals foraging close by.

But what if it wasn't an animal or the wind? It could be more of Marcus's men coming to burn Thomas's place down or just kill

200

everyone. Considering what happened at Cathy's place, it wasn't out of the realm of possibility.

Both dogs stared at the dense line of trees. They scooted forward a few paces while barking under their breath. Muscles rippled through Butch's chest as short ruffs fled his snout.

Russell ventured down the stretch of porch to the edge of the cabin. He squinted and surveyed the area for any movement within the thicket that surrounded the bases of the trees.

It was hard to pierce through the wall of vegetation, but he didn't get the sense that a person was lurking beyond the barrier of bushes and shrubs since the dogs didn't venture over there.

"Come on, guys. Let's head back inside," he ordered.

Both animals ignored Russell as they continued to skim over the area. Max turned away and trotted over to the porch while Butch remained deadlocked on the greenery.

Max approached the front door and sat on his haunches, waiting to be let in. Butch grunted and snarled for a moment longer before retreating to the porch.

Russell skimmed over the trees as he headed back to the entrance of the cabin. The nagging feeling of something not being right stuck to him like glue.

He opened the door. The dogs flooded into the house in a mad dash. They slipped and lost their balance as their wet paws struggled to find traction on the planks of wood.

Thomas and Cathy were sitting by the fireplace conversing. It didn't sound as heated as the night before. There were no raised voices or looks of frustration on either of their faces.

Russell took a few steps forward, then paused. He turned toward the closed door and stared.

"What's wrong?" Cathy inquired.

"Not sure. It's probably nothing," Russell responded. "Could just be me being paranoid given all that has happened."

Thomas shifted in his chair. "Did you see someone out there?"

Russell shook his head. "No. The dogs were fixed on something in the bushes off to the west of the house. I couldn't see any movement because of all the bushes and trees, but whatever was over there had their attention."

Cathy glanced at Thomas with a concerned look. She gulped. "Marcus hasn't threatened you or anything like that, has he?"

Thomas thought about it for a second. His hand rubbed the gray stubble on his box chin as he thought back. "Not really. I mean, his boys have stopped by to talk about my property, inquiring if I'd be willing to sell and such. They didn't try anything like they did at your place if that's what you mean. Maybe they haven't gotten to that point. I've told them time and again that I'm not interested. So far, they haven't pressed the issue. To be honest, I think they've been out here snooping around at night, though. I haven't seen anyone, but Butch gets wound up tight at times and antsy. That's why I was a bit defensive when you first arrived. I had plans of speaking with the sheriff about it, just so he's aware."

"Why didn't you tell me they were talking to you as well?" Cathy snapped with a bit of anger to her voice.

Thomas shrugged. "I didn't want to bother you with my problems. Besides, like I said, they weren't really harassing me. Not like they were you."

Cathy lowered her head, shaking it in frustration. "Well, I don't feel right leaving now knowing that they're bothering you as well."

"It'll be fine," Thomas countered as Butch sat next to his chair. "I've got my bud here to protect me. Like we just talked about, when we go into town, we'll stop by the sheriff's office and lay everything out. We can at least get the process going for them to look into what happened at your place."

Russell stood just outside of the living room watching the two of them. It wasn't his place to interject his thoughts on the matter. His main and only concern was getting back to Sarah. If they tapped him for his thoughts, he'd fill them in. Other than that, it was their business to handle.

Cathy stood from her chair. Her palms rested on her hips as she shot Russell a quick glance. "Let's go ahead and get ready to leave since we're stopping by the sheriff's office. Hopefully, they won't be too tied up with this blackout."

"Sounds good," Thomas said relieved. "I think getting the process going will help out a bunch. Let me grab a few things, and we'll be on our way."

Butch flanked Thomas as he walked around the couch and past Russell. He gave a simple nod as he disappeared down the dark hallway that led to his bedroom at the other end of the cabin.

"I can't believe that dirt bag is bothering Thomas as well," Cathy mumbled.

"Why does he want Thomas's place as well?" Russell inquired.

"Control. Power. His family never owned any portion of Thomas's land, but it seems like he's making a play for it, regardless. There have been talks of possible commercial development, but not sure what that would entail. All I know is that we're not leaving. Even with what happened to my place, I'll rebuild. It's still my land, and that piece of crap isn't going to get it. Ever."

"This Marcus Wright seems like a real peach. I'm surprised the authorities have allowed him to continue harassing everyone."

Cathy rubbed Max's head. A scowl formed on her face for a split second before she shook the disgruntled expression away. "I think the sheriff is in his back pocket. With this being such a small town with limited income potential versus' the bigger cities, some jump at the chance to get that money. He has the funds to pay off whoever he needs to and do what he wants. That, and he employs a lot of the towns people since he owns a majority of the businesses. Most of the people who live around here aren't wealthy and depend on those jobs. They turn a blind eye, and keep their noses out of his business to avoid his wrath. I don't do that since I'm not under his thumb, and that makes me a prime target. It's all about control at the end of the day."

Russell nodded, remembering her saying as much about the sheriff. A crooked cop was the last thing they needed. He hoped she was overexaggerating and that wasn't the case.

Thomas walked up the hallway with Butch at his side. A rifle was draped over one shoulder and a dark green pack over the other. The limp he had the night before had all but vanished. "Are we ready to go?"

Cathy noticed the gear he was hauling. She gave him a puzzled stare. "What's with the rifle and bug out bag?"

He dropped the rucksack to the floor which hit with a heavy thud.

"It's for Russell. Figured he could use it while you're on the road. Who knows what things are like out there? I've got another one stowed away I can use if I need to." Thomas glanced at the rifle. "This is just in case we run into trouble. Better to be safe than sorry, right?"

"Hopefully, we won't need them," Cathy said. "But, if they try anything again, I won't hesitate to drop them where they stand."

Thomas nodded in agreement.

Powerless World

Russell was a bit out of his depth with what was happening. He was just a city boy who had somehow been thrust into the middle of an escalating ordeal that wasn't getting any better. Still, he had their backs and would do what was needed to get home.

Cathy grabbed her gear and rifle from behind the chair she was standing next to. She lugged the pack onto her shoulder and moved toward the front door.

Max followed as Russell stepped out of their way.

"You should be good to go." Thomas nudged the rucksack with his boot. "It's got most of your basic essentials. Flashlight, batteries, rope, first aid kit, etc."

Russell retrieved the bag from the floor. It was heavy, but not too bad. He slung the gear over his shoulder, then nodded. "I appreciate it."

"It's not a problem. Happy to help out." Thomas looked past him to the entrance of the cabin. "What is it?"

Russell stepped to the side and noticed Cathy standing in the doorway. She was frozen in place. Her head moved from side to side as if she had spotted something.

Max growled beside her, his rigid stance confirming that danger was lurking beyond the walls of the cabin.

"Max, back." Cathy retreated into the cabin along with Max. She pulled the door to, leaving it cracked just enough to look outside. She dropped the bag to the floor, then slipped the rifle free of her arm. "I spotted movement in the trees and it wasn't an animal. We've got company."

CHAPTER TWENTY-FIVE

SARAH

Rick's thick-soled boots hammered the concrete at a good clip. Sarah stayed a few paces behind for fear of being left in the lurch.

They had attracted unwanted attention a block back from an SUV that rolled through the lightless intersection. It slowed to a crawl as they hoofed it down the sidewalk. A voice shouted at their backs from the vehicle.

"What do they want?" Sarah asked through panted breath.

"Don't know. Don't care. Keep moving and don't stop. We're almost there." Rick's voice was strained from breathing heavily as he kept his focus dead ahead.

Sarah peered over her shoulder, searching for the trolling stark white SUV. She couldn't lay eyes on it which worried her.

Powerless World

Rick's head moved on a swivel, checking each building and car they passed. The Glock remained nestled within the waistband of his jeans, as did hers, for now.

He slowed his pace and dipped behind the corner of a building.

Sarah fell in line behind Rick and hit the ground. She deflated against the brick wall. Her shoulders sagged with exhaustion. The lack of proper sleep, fluids, and a decent meal was taking its toll and her body was fighting to keep up.

Rick toed the edge of the building with his back flush against the wall. He leaned to the side and peered out to the street. "I don't see them. Looks like they might have moved on."

Thank God. Sarah's lungs burned, as did her legs. A cramp fixed in her side as she pressed her palm to her ribs. "If I'd known the end of the world was going to happen, I would've worn different shoes and clothes."

"Yeah, well, hindsight is 20/20, isn't it?" Rick countered. "Those people in that SUV could've been all right, but I wouldn't take the chance. You just never know what people are going to do. That's me, though."

Sarah hated to think like that, but it was a mixed bag for her. Most of what she had witnessed proved his point.

The crumbling of society had hit its stride and it showed no signs of faltering anytime soon.

"So, where are we going?" she posed. "I'm assuming you have some sort of vehicle, right?"

Rick brushed the back of his hand across his moist brow, then flicked his wrist. "Yeah. My car's in the shop down on the corner. It's been ready for a bit, but I haven't had the cash to get it out."

Sarah glanced down the street to the painted white building on the corner. The large, unlit sign in the parking lot looked rusted and faded. It was hard to read from where she was. "So, you've got the money now to get it out?"

"Not exactly."

"Then how do you plan on us getting it?"

"I know the guy who owns it. He owes me a favor for doing some P.I. work on his ex-wife some years back. I cut him a deal for the job. He said he'd hook me up when I needed it."

"Did that entail doing the work for free?"

"Probably not, but we'll hash that out when we get there. Come on."

Rick and Sarah bolted from the cover of the building to the row of cars that lined the street. They kept low to the ground and out of sight.

He craned his neck, and peered over the sedan they were hunched next to, searching for the white SUV or any surly types who might be lurking in the area.

Sarah surveyed the sidewalk, making sure they weren't being stalked.

Rick tapped her shoulder, then nodded. "Looks clear from here."

He skirted around the bumper of the sedan to the gap between the truck that was parked behind the car. A moment of hesitation was all that was given before Rick stood up.

They darted across the street to the sidewalk and kept moving in the direction of the garage.

The buildings they passed hadn't suffered any looting or other damage. Doors were shut and windows intact. For now, they had been spared.

The hint of smoke hadn't waned. The sky remained murky and painted with strokes of dark gray. It looked similar to when a thunderstorm was rolling in, but thunder couldn't be heard.

Rick paused before passing each alley or nook between the buildings. He scoped them out with a quick glance, then moved on.

Brick gave way to a wall of chain link fencing that ran to the edge of the garage. Coiled barbed wire was fastened to the top of the fence.

Scores of cars littered the yard. Some looked in decent condition while others were spotted in rust and sat on tireless rims.

A large lock with a thick steel chain was looped around the two sections of the gates. Rick grabbed the lock and tugged as he looked over the sea of metal.

It didn't budge. The chain rattled and struck the stranded steel wire and poles of the gate.

"Must be inside still." He let go of the lock and turned toward the garage.

They ran down the remaining length of the fence and stopped at the corner of the white concrete structure.

Sarah checked their six. They were still in the clear with no movement detected on the street or from the buildings across from them.

Rick peered from the edge of the garage, then slid down the front of the business. The large windows within the roll up doors had a black film over them. A few spots within the glass were free of the dark tint.

He leaned in close, with his hand above his brow, checking all three stalls as he moved down to the entrance of the building. "There it is."

"Is there anyone inside?"

Rick shook his head. "Not that I can see. It's pretty dark inside. I was only able to spot my car by the shred of light that's hitting the license plate."

The grumbling of an engine stirred down the street.

Sarah turned and searched for the vehicle. The white SUV sprung to mind as she stepped away from the garage. She trained her ear, trying to pinpoint where it was coming from.

Rick grabbed Sarah by the arm and pulled her toward the main entrance. He peered through the grime-coated glass to the dark office.

He grabbed the silver handle and pulled. It opened with little effort, and they funneled into the building. They took cover behind the wall near the entrance.

"You see who it is?" Sarah inquired.

Rick reached up and locked the door. "Not yet."

He watched the parking lot, craning his neck as he searched for the vehicle.

Sarah skimmed over the waiting area of the shop. It was empty, which was odd considering that the door was unlocked. She didn't detect any movement or voices from the ether.

The large counter in front of them ran the width of the space. A single door in the corner led out into the shop. There were a few offices along the wall that were dark with the blinds closed. "Doesn't seem like your friend is here, much less anyone else."

Rick stood and backed away from the entrance. "Allen probably went home to his kid. Not sure why he didn't lock up, though. I can't imagine him not doing that."

Sarah skimmed over the papers that carpeted the tile floor. "Unless your friend is always this messy, someone could've broken into his shop and trashed the place."

Rick skimmed over the disheveled mess. His boots kicked up the loose papers as he sighed, then said, "Looks like it. Every time I've stopped by, his shop was always immaculate. Well, as clean as one can be for an automotive repair shop. I know he has some guys who are pretty messy, though. At least, that's what he has told me."

A black sedan barreled through the parking lot and came to a screeching halt near the entrance. Rick pointed to the counter as he drew his Glock.

Sarah bolted for the gap on the far side of the office. Her feet plowed through the papers on the floor as she skirted the edge of the counter.

The palm of her hand slid over the top as quick breaths escaped her lips. A dark figure laid prone on its side on the floor. Both arms were stretched out toward the wall and bound together.

A panicked scream boomed from Sarah's mouth, and she clapped her hand over her lips.

"What's wrong?" Rick inquired as he chambered a round. He glanced over to Sarah who stood frozen in place.

"There's a body over here," Sarah muttered.

"A what?" Rick countered. "Did you say a body?"

Sarah nodded as she took a step back.

The car out front killed the engine.

Rick peered through the glass door, then back to Sarah. "Are they alive?"

"I don't know. He's either dead or unconscious because he's not moving." Sarah nudged the bearded man's boot with her shoe. He didn't move or flinch from the contact.

"Shit," Rick groused under his breath.

"Yeah. I know. Someone for sure messed this guy up. I hope he's not dead."

Rick retreated to the far side of the counter where Sarah was. "We've got four guys out there standing around. I don't think they're friendlies." He hovered over her shoulder, and stared at the body.

"What makes you think that?" Sarah shot him a concerned glance as he squinted and leaned forward.

"You can just tell with some people. I've been around enough low life's and degenerates to know when trouble is lurking. Those four goons out there aren't anything we want to be a part of." Rick shuffled Sarah to the side and got a closer look at the body. "Can't be sure, but it looks like one of Allen's employees. Bill or Bobby or something like that. I only met him briefly."

A shadow from outside played over the wall near the entrance to the shop. Both Sarah and Rick dropped to the floor in a blink. He shushed her in a low tone as they crouched in the darkness.

The door to the entrance of the building rattled. Rick held the Glock firm in his grasp as he stood up. He peered over the counter as Sarah wrestled the Glock from the waistband of her trousers.

"Allen. You in there, bud?" an agitated voice beckoned. Fists pounded the glass door hard enough to rattle Sarah. She flinched with each strike. "We stopped by earlier to catch up. Spoke with one of your employees, who wasn't too helpful. Your extensions have run out and Kinnerk wants his money in full. It's past time to pay up on your debt."

"Sounds like your friend, Allen, is in deep with the wrong people," Sarah observed. "Which means, now we are for just being here."

Powerless World

CHAPTER TWENTY-SIX

RUSSELL

Russell spotted flashes of movement through the blinds covering the front windows of the cabin,. He counted at least three men shuffling for cover. It was hard to tell if they were armed or not. Considering their covert tactics, it was safe to assume so.

"Company?" Thomas parroted. "Mr. Wright's men?"

Cathy cracked the door open a hair more, then craned her neck. "That's what I'm thinking. Not sure who else would be skulking in the woods around your property. Maybe they're coming to finish what they started at my place. Marcus knows we're friends. That, or he could be coming after you. Who knows?"

Max lowered to the floor in a crouched posture. His ears folded back onto his head. The hairs along his spine stood on end as he growled.

Butch acted much the same way. The dogs were spooked and didn't care for the trespassers.

"You got another way out of here?" Russell probed. The last thing he was looking to do was get into another altercation.

Thomas clutched his rifle tighter. His boney fingers turned a milky white as his long, distant gaze loomed out through the windows.

Russell couldn't tell what was going on inside his head, or what he was contemplating.

"Uh, yeah." Thomas turned and looked away from the window, then pointed down the hallway. "There's a way out through the laundry room that leads to the car port where my Explorer is parked."

"I say we slip through the laundry room. Load up in the Explorer, and get the hell out of here before the shit hits the fan," Russell suggested.

Cathy moved the barrel of her rifle through the gap between the door and jamb. It was tilted up toward the sky.

A single round fired off.

The dogs held their ground and kept their defensive stance.

"That's far enough," Cathy shouted with a hoarse growl. "If you value your lives, don't come any closer."

Russell watched as she kept her rifle in view of the men beyond the walls. Her finger hugged the trigger as she peered around the jamb of the door.

"Here. Take this." Thomas pressed a pistol against Russell's chest. "It's already got a round chambered and the magazine is stocked."

Russell dipped his chin, then took the dark-gray pistol. The cool steel grip fit in the palm of his hand nicely.

"You know how to use one of those, right?" Thomas inquired.

"Yeah." He wasn't looking to fire the pistol unless he had to. Killing someone wasn't on his list of things to accomplish that day. It was viewed as more of a deterrent than anything else. If it had to be done to protect himself, or the lives of others, so be it, but that wasn't the goal.

"They're not backing down," Cathy advised. "I can still see them out there moving within the trees and bushes. Looks like they might be trying to box us in." She glanced back to both Russell and Thomas who stood at the ready with their weapons fixed in their hands.

Russell pointed to the hallway. "We should fall back now while we can. Load up in the Explorer and hall ass to town. With the phones dead, we can't call this in, and there could be more waiting out there."

Thomas stared at his home with a frown that twisted to an angry scowl in a blink. "As much as I don't want to tuck tail and leave, he's right. We need to get out of here while we can. We'll deal with that dirtbag and his hoodlums soon enough."

Gunfire erupted from outside of the cabin. Multiple reports sounded off at once. The rounds pelted the log cabin without pause.

Cathy slammed the door shut and took cover behind the wall. She stooped down and huddled next to the entrance as Max sat prone on his stomach at her feet.

Both Thomas and Russell hit the floor as round after round tore through the cabin. They covered their heads and stayed low while the hailstorm of gunfire hammered the house.

Glass shattered.

Wood splintered.

The stuffing from the furniture fluttered in the air as the fabric was torn open.

"Damn sons of bitches," Thomas raged. "This is my house, damn it."

He scrambled to get to his feet as he mumbled a slew of obscenities through pursed lips.

"Stay down," Russell demanded as he grabbed at Thomas's arm.

Thomas jerked his arm free of Russell's hand and stormed across the living room with his rifle fixed in his grasp.

Cathy waved Thomas off, shouting at him to take cover, but he didn't listen.

A stray round busted through the front door and caught him in the arm. The impact turned him sideways and sent him stumbling.

"Thomas," Cathy shouted.

The rifle fell from his hands as he crashed into the wall that sectioned off the other room. He palmed the wound and grumbled in pain through clenched teeth as he crumbled to the floor.

Cathy darted to his side in a flash.

Russell scrambled off the floor and scurried to the injured old man.

"What the hell were you thinking?" Cathy scolded. "You could've been killed."

Thomas removed his hand from his upper bicep. It looked like the bullet had caught the outside edge of the muscle. "I'm fine. I think it only grazed me."

"Doesn't matter, you crazy coot. You're lucky it didn't hit someplace vital," Cathy barked.

The gunfire waned.

Silence fell over the cabin as they knelt next to Thomas.

"Where are the keys?" Russell asked.

Thomas rolled to his side, then pointed to his coat. "In my pocket here."

Footfalls creaked over the porch as Russell dug his hand into the pocket of Thomas's coat. He fished out the keys as the shadow of a figure loomed in front of the window.

Cathy spun toward the entrance and shouldered her weapon. She squeezed the trigger as the doorknob spun.

Fire spat from the muzzle. A white flash glared in Russell's eyes as the report hammered his head.

The round punched through the door with ease. A dense thud hit the planks of wood outside, followed by a howl.

"Let's go," Russell ordered.

Cathy locked the door, then retrieved her bag from the floor.

Russell helped Thomas to his feet. "You good?"

He tilted his head as blood trickled out from around his fingers. "Yeah. Just hurts like a son of a bitch."

Cathy scooped up Thomas's rifle and darted past them without breaking her stride. Max stayed on her six as they barreled down the hallway toward the laundry room.

Russell motioned for Thomas to get going. "Go. Get in the Explorer."

Thomas staggered past Russell as more boards from the porch gave their warning. Through the windows, Russell spotted movement. Figures peered inside through the busted glass, trying to gauge the situation.

He reached down and grabbed the straps of the rucksack as he backed away. The pistol trained at the entrance, then to the windows on either side of the door.

The doorknob shuddered.

Powerless World

Russell gulped as he drifted back down the hallway. He peered over his shoulder and watched as Thomas vanished around the corner of the laundry room.

Loud voices boomed from beyond the porch. Angered and enraged, they grew louder.

The door shuddered under the weight of something heavy slamming into it. Russell didn't fire the pistol as he back peddled past the kitchen.

Two more strikes and the door gave way. The jamb splintered and cracked. The door smashed into the wall. Any glass that remained within the window shattered and littered the floor.

A large, burly man stomped his way inside the house with a shotgun clutched in his bear-sized hands. Beady eyes scanned over the cabin from under the black beanie on his round head. He spotted Russell down the hall and trained the barrel in his direction.

"They're fleeing out the side of the house," he shouted.

Russell fired at the burly man's legs. Two rounds popped off, one right after the other. Each found their mark in his knee cap and upper thigh.

"Aww," he yelled in agony as he stumbled across the floor. His shotgun fired at the ceiling. His legs gave out, and he hit face first.

Another intruder rushed into the cabin with his pistol drawn. His identity was concealed by the skull face shield he wore.

Russell stepped inside the laundry room as the intruder opened fire. Bullets whizzed past the doorway like a swarm of angry wasps.

Cathy crouched next to the Explorer and returned fire. "Come on, Russell, Move it."

Russell stumbled out of the laundry room and into the car port.

She stood up and moved around the rear of the SUV with her rifle shouldered. A head poked out from the side of the cabin and the man returned fire.

Russell ducked and wrenched the driver's side door open. He crammed the rucksack in the back seat with Thomas. Both dogs were in the far seat behind him, barking and growling at the assailants.

Cathy hopped inside and slammed the door.

Russell scaled the off-road beast and settled into the rich leather seat.

"How are you doing back there?" Cathy looked at the backseat where Thomas was slouched.

The palm of his hand pressed against the gunshot. "I'm good."

Skull-mask materialized from the hallway with his weapon trained at the Explorer.

Russell fired, sending the goon scurrying back to the hallway for cover.

"I hope you can drive good," Cathy grumbled as she checked her sideview mirror.

"Yeah. I got this." Russell fired up the Explorer. The engine grumbled to life. He shifted into reverse and punched the gas.

Tires squealed as the hulking beast barreled out of the car port. Russell tossed his arm over Cathy's seat. He peered to the back window, trying to see around the dogs that blocked his view.

A figure dashed from the corner of the house and stepped in front of the SUV. The man fired round after round at the Explorer. Russell hit the brakes as the window cracked.

Powerless World

The rear of the vehicle slammed into the armed gunman, knocking him hard to the ground.

Skull-mask emerged from the cabin and opened fire. The incoming rounds punched through the tempered glass windows.

"Son of a–" Russell shouted as both he and Cathy ducked.

He worked the brake and shifted the Explorer into drive. He torqued the steering wheel clockwise. His foot pressed the gas pedal to the floor. Chunks of rock fired from under the spinning tires like a hailstorm of bullets.

"Go, go," Cathy urged.

The SUV raced up the rock driveway toward the main road. Russell kept both hands on the steering wheel as he checked the sideview mirror.

Skull-mask rushed to his fallen man's aid. He pointed at the Explorer, then yelled at the house.

"When you hit the road, hook a right, and watch out," Cathy shouted.

An older model red Chevy Dually pulled into the driveway, blocking their escape. Russell spun the steering wheel, sending the steel beast barreling through the grass.

The front end of the Explorer dumped into the ditch that lined the edge of the road. The large, thick-treaded tires ate the dirt and scaled the embankment with ease. The SUV bulldozed through the bushes and small shrubs that lined the road.

Russell kept his foot mashed to the floorboard as the tires found the main road. The Explorer gained speed on the smooth, even blacktop.

The Dually was in pursuit and gaining fast. The rusted grill and bumper drew closer to the rear of the Explorer.

"How far is the town?" Russell asked through panted breath.

His heart hammered his ribs. Beads of sweat poured from his scalp and raced down his flushed face. The back of his hand brushed the nervousness away as he concentrated on the winding road.

"Maybe four or five miles. Don't let up on the gas," Cathy fired back.

The Dually nudged the Explorer which sent the SUV swerving from side to side on the narrow, one-lane road. Russell turned the steering wheel, trying to correct their course.

The tires ripped through the dirt on the side of the road that dropped off in a steep valley filled with trees.

Russell straightened the Explorer as the Dually darted into the other lane. Both vehicles ran neck and neck through blinding curves and winding roads. The thought of an oncoming car riddled Russell with fear, but he remained in control.

"These people are insane." Russell glanced through the window at the masked men in the large truck.

The driver jerked the wheel, sending the 6,000 plus pound behemoth crashing into them. Tortured metal groaned as both vehicles ground against each other.

"They're trying to run us off the road," Cathy shouted.

The Dually pulled away and readied for another strike. Russell had to act fast. He wasn't sure they could withstand another blow.

An idea gelled in his brain. Something he had only seen in the movies. He was unsure if it would work, but he had to try. "Everyone, hold on."

"Why?" Cathy countered.

"You'll see."

A sharp curve which was coming up fast. The truck went wide, then darted across the road. Russell punched the brake.

Powerless World

Cathy palmed the dash as they were thrown forward. The tires squealed and stopped on a dime. The Dually rubbed the front of the Explorer and kept going.

The truck dumped over the side of the road and vanished from sight.

Russell placed the SUV into park, threw open the door, and jumped down to the asphalt. He raced around the front of the Explorer to the side of the road.

The Dually had obliterated a swath of trees. Its frame was a contorted mess. Smoke plumed from the engine. He couldn't see any movement within the wreckage.

Cathy hammered the side of the passenger door.

Russell backed away from the edge of the road and made for the driver's side. He climbed into the SUV and plopped down in the seat.

"Well?" Cathy inquired.

He slammed the door, then put the Explorer into drive. The weight of knowing that those men probably died weighed heavy on his mind, but he had to stay focused. He shook his head, then said, "Looks like we're in the clear, for now, at least."

Cathy nodded. "Good. Get us to the sheriff's station, now."

Derek Shupert

CHAPTER TWENTY-SEVEN

SARAH

The goons outside the building grew impatient. They hammered the glass door without pause. It rattled inside the jamb.

"Allen, stop dicking around. I know you're in there. You weren't at your place, and this shithole is the only other dump you'd come to."

Rick scoured the shelves under the counter for his keys. He fished through the file trays and other paperwork to no avail. "Allen normally keeps the keys with the paperwork in packets once the repairs had been finished. He stores them below the register."

Sarah kept a watchful eye on the door as Rick grew impatient.

"Damn it." he growled. "I can't see a thing down here?"

Their phones were kept off. The light from the screens would only give them away to the goons outside.

"Where else could he have kept them?" Sarah asked.

Rick shrugged. "I have no clue."

"We better find them fast. They're losing their patience out there." Sarah stood up near the cash register, making sure to stay hidden behind it. The shadows from the men had vanished from the wall behind her. She peered over the counter and to the side of the register.

The henchmen were nowhere to be seen. Their sedan was still out front, though. Where did they go?

"He may have left the keys out in the shop. If we can't find them, I'll just hotwire the damn thing." Rick stepped around the dead body and squeezed past Sarah.

She kept an eye out for the henchmen as Rick cracked open the door. He slipped through, then waved for her to follow.

Sarah backed through the door as a shadow washed over the wall from the entrance. She pulled the door to and moved away.

Blinding darkness filled the garage. The smell of oil and rubber permeated the air. Sarah squinted, trying to pierce the blackness that blanketed the shop. Minus the few rays of light that bled through the small openings within the film-covered windows and along the rails of the roll up door helped some in navigating the dark garage.

"My car is in the second stall," he whispered. "Stay close and be quiet."

"Go check and see if the keys are in your car," Sarah said. "I'm going to look around here for a moment to see if I can find anything. They've got to be here somewhere."

Rick looked to the bay doors, then rubbed his chin. "All right. Just hurry up."

The roll up doors rattled. They lifted off the ground a scant inch, allowing more light in to battle the darkness.

Bickering voices loomed from outside. Shadows could be seen on the ground below the metal door.

It dropped, severing the light. From the agitated quarrel of the henchmen, Sarah feared they would breach the office soon. They had to move fast.

Rick quickly navigated the shop as Sarah scavenged for the keys. It would've been easier, and faster, if she could've used the flashlight on her phone, but doing so would've only drawn attention.

A loud clanging noise filled the garage, followed by Rick cussing under his breath. He had run into a chest that sent tools clattering off the cement.

"There's someone in there," a deep baritone voice boomed from outside the stall.

"Christ. Come on," Rick urged as he ran for his car.

Fists pounded the stall door. It lifted off the ground an inch or two. Gunshots fired from the office, followed by the shattering of glass.

Sarah flinched as she looked about the garage. They were surrounded. The bay doors continued to roll up as footfalls from the main office hammered her ears.

A light manifested from the interior of the car, illuminating Rick as he slipped inside the driver's seat. They weren't going to be able to pull away before the men got to them. She had no desire to fight the strangers who were invading the shop, but she wasn't going to allow them to steal her life, or Rick's.

She pulled the Glock from her waistband and trained it at the bay door. Her finger squeezed the trigger without any hesitation.

The Glock barked a harsh report within the garage. The single round struck the bicep of the man lifting the bay door up. He let go of the sheet metal bottom and palmed his arm. He scurried for cover and vanished from her sight.

"What the hell was that?" Rick shouted as he got out of the car with his Glock in hand. Light from outside flooded into the garage as he turned to the opened bay door.

"Just worry about the car," Sarah shouted back.

He hesitated for a moment, staring outside before he slipped back inside his car.

Sarah grabbed the doorknob of the door that led into the office and cracked it open. Her back pressed to the wall as she tilted her head to the side while still keeping a vigilant eye on the open bay door. "I don't know who you are, but if you come any closer, I will shoot you dead. That I can promise you."

The crunching of glass filled her ears as a figure raced for the door. Sarah checked the bay door, but didn't spot any movement there either.

"You're going to regret doing this," an angered voice called out. "Tell Allen he's a dead man, and so are you."

The slamming of car doors played from outside of the mechanic's shop. Sarah made her way through the garage to the open bay door. Her shoulder pressed to the cinderblock wall as she scooted to the edge.

An engine revved, followed by squealing tires. A car tore past the open bay and made for the street.

Sarah breathed a sigh of relief, then lowered the pistol. Oddly enough, her hands were completely still. She was glad the men had retreated and decided not to test her resolve. They would have found out how formidable she could have been.

Rick's car found new life. The engine coughed, but started just the same. He hopped out with the Glock trained ahead of him as he made his way toward her. He craned his neck and peered to the front of the garage.

"So the keys were inside?" Sarah asked.

"Nope. Had to hotwire the damn thing." Rick stared a bit longer before looking back to her. "Are you ok?"

Sarah nodded. "Yeah. I'm good."

Rick lowered the Glock to his side. "That was brave what you did. Foolish, but brave. They could've killed you."

"They didn't, though, and we're all right. I had to do something to buy us some time. They didn't sound like they just wanted to chat," she countered.

"True, but it was still brazen."

Sarah changed the subject. "Are we good to get out of here."

Rick nodded, then glanced at his car. "Yeah."

He turned and headed for the driver's side as Sarah walked past the rear of the vehicle.

Perhaps her actions were rash, but Sarah didn't see any other options other than what she did. Fight or die. It was as simple as that.

They had skirted danger, but they were not out of the clear yet. More threats would loom large in the city and they had to be ready for anything.

Sarah wasn't looking for trouble, but if it came her way, she'd fight like hell to protect herself, and those around her.

Derek Shupert

ABOUT THE AUTHOR

Derek Shupert is an emerging Science Fiction Author known for his captivating dystopian storylines and post-apocalyptic-laden plots. With various books and anthologies underway, he is also the author of the Afflicted series and Sentry Squad.

Outside of the fantastical world of sci-fi, Derek serves as the Vice President at Woodforest National Bank. During his free time, he enjoys reading, exercising, and watching apocalyptic movies and TV shows like Mad Max and The Walking Dead. Above all, he is a family man who cherishes nothing more than quality time spent with his loved ones.

To find out more about Derek Shupert and his forthcoming publications, visit his official website at **www.derekshupert.com.**

Printed in Great Britain
by Amazon

52845841R00144